EDGE

A town terrified into submission; a sheriff that respects no law but his own; and an axe-wielding, crazed band of vigilantes. Edge knows that to survive he must destroy a vicious gang of hired killers. But it is never easy for the man who treads a path of violence. There are always victims awash in the bloody wake . . . some innocent, some deserving of their fate. And Edge cannot stop on his collision course with destiny to find out which side a man is on.

WARNING

This story is not for
the fainthearted reader.

The Edge Series

EDGE

THE HATED

BY

GEORGE G. GILMAN

PINNACLE BOOKS • NEW YORK CITY

EDGE: THE HATED

Copyright © 1974 by George G. Gilman

A Pinnacle Books edition, published by special arrangement with New English Library, Limited, London.

ISBN: 0-523-00560-1

First printing, March 1975

Printed in the United States of America

PINNACLE BOOKS, INC.
275 Madison Avenue
New York, N.Y. 10016

For C.S.
with a promise that—unlike Edge—I will not alter
the way folks look

CHAPTER ONE

THE pine trees grew tall and close together, their dark green foliage acting as a filter for the hot, bright sunlight of noon. Thus the needle-covered floor of the forest was cool, a condition which was appreciated by the grey gelding and the man who rode the horse. Both rider and mount showed signs of a long, hard ride but now they were taking it easy as reins and heels made no demands: the gelding allowed to set his own pace and choose a meandering course among the trees.

They had been in the forest for more than an hour and covered no more than two miles in a generally northwestern direction. There had been just one stop—for the gelding to drink from a cool, sweetwater spring while the man filled his two canteens and rolled some cigarettes. He smoked one of these now, hanging it from a corner of his mouth as he surveyed the way ahead. The view was the same as it had always been since he had steered the gelding into the great forest spread over the foothills of the Rocky Mountains of Montana Territory's Continental Divide: a seemingly solid wall of Ponderosa pine trunks that appeared as an impassable barrier until the angle of vision changed and the gelding swung to left or right around the trees.

But, when the man had finished smoking the cigarette and carefully squeezed out the fire between thumb and forefinger before dropping the butt, the terrain ahead had taken on a different aspect. The plateau across which the man had been traveling since entering the forest came to an end and a valley was opened up; the ground on either side rising sharply. There were breaks in the trees at points where the terrain reared almost vertically and wind and rain had eroded the soil clear down to the rock. In the valley there were more breaks, but these were man-made: ugly scars of brown, black and yellow slashed against the green skin of the land. The brown of earth, the black of rotted needles and the yellow of pine stumps.

The valley sloped gently down from where the man halted the gelding. Then, a mile ahead, it rose like a green ocean swell and appeared to fall sharply on the far side. The sun poured brilliant light down into the valley and, many miles distant beyond the crest of the rise, it was reflected in vivid white off the snow-capped jaggedness of the Divide mountain tops. A patch of blue—much deeper than the insipid color of the sun-washed sky—showed the location of a high-country lake.

The man looked at the awe-inspiring magnificence of the vista with a cold indifference and clucked the gelding forward. The drop down into the valley was less than two hundred feet, but the slope was a steep one and the rider took firmer control of his mount. He kept the animal on a diagonal course, across the face of the slope. On occasions the treacherous springiness of the pine needles slid from beneath the hooves of the gelding and the animal was on the verge of panic. But a tight rein and soft-spoken words held him in check. The lofty pines continued to shield the ground from the direct heat of the sun as it inched into the downward slide of afternoon. But the man sweated freely and white lather foamed on the gelding's flanks in the cool, green shade. For the coolness among the trees was more in the mind than the air and the merest exertion erupted salty moisture from wide open pores. It was that kind of summer: only relatively cool in the shade because out in the open where a man cast a shadow the heat threatened to fry his eyes.

At the foot of the incline the man kept the horse moving and sucked water slowly from one of his canteens. It was lukewarm but he drank to replace lost moisture rather than to slake thirst. He poured some into the cupped palm of a hand and rubbed his forehead, washing off the stinging beads of sweat before they dropped into his eyes.

The easy pace along the floor of the broadening valley reduced the body temperatures of both man and animal and by the time they reached the trail they were again cocooned in a pretense of coolness. The trail appeared abruptly and at first it was only discernible for what it was because of the wagon-wide, unnaturally straight clearway through the trees. It began—or more likely, ended—two hundred feet from the foot of the slope and the fact of its existence did not surprise the man. For the men who had felled the timber so haphazardly in the valley needed some kind of road to haul it out.

That had been a long time ago, for the wheel ruts which would have made the trail obvious were now filled with the rotted needles of several years; so that the way through the trees appeared evenly carpeted by the detritus of many falls. Because of the frugal narrowness of the man-made thoroughfare, it had been concealed from above and the pines rearing up on either side continued to shade the ground. At intervals along the trail, spurs veered off to the left and right, forcing a right of way to the areas where the old lumber operations had been active. Where the ground began to rise in the manner of an ocean breaker between the steep sides of the valley, there was a half acre or so of stripped forest immediately beside the main trail. The passage of time since the lumber camp had been worked was very evident here. More than one harsh Montana winter had ravaged the signs which man had left of his former presence. And these comprised more than just the moss-encrusted stumps of felled pines. In one corner of the stripped area there was the foundation of a small cabin with just a single wall left standing. Incredibly, one pane of glass remained unbroken in the window. Grass grew up through the cracks in the collapsed, rotten roof and other three walls. A wheel-less wagon was canted across a tree stump nearby. Against it rested an ax and a broken wheel. Ax blade and wheelrim were dull red with rust.

The man riding the grey gelding took in all this with the same brand of impassive detachment he had showed to every other vista displayed for him. It was there, offered him nothing good or bad and he accepted it as automatically as the air he breathed. Whereas another man might have sensed a pang of melancholia at viewing this scene of a forest raped and abandoned, this man did not. Just as he had been singularly unimpressed by the magnificence of the vista from the high ground: a breathtaking panorama which would probably have caused another man to contemplate the wonders of nature.

But such emotional reflections required an ability which this man no longer possessed: an ability to experience normal human feelings. A little more than a decade previously, this man had been as well equipped with humanity as most. But the life fate had decreed for him since that earlier time had robbed him of virtually every quality that separates the thinking man from the most vicious of the wild animals.

Now, riding in apparent relaxation up the slope of the trail, he did not at first glance appear different in any great degree from other men. He was tall—six feet three inches—and gave an impression of lean sparseness in his build: although almost two hundred pounds was evenly and solidly distributed over his frame. His features were of the kind that could be termed either handsome or extremely unlovely, depending upon the eye of the beholder. His own eyes were of the clearest blue, hooded and showing little of themselves between slitted lids. The glinting brightness of the eyes seemed strangely at odds with his other features: high cheekbones, hawk-like nose, thin-lipped mouth and thick black hair which reached down in a tangle to brush his shoulders. But then the sculptured firmness of his jaw line seemed to strike an affinity with the eyes: and neither suggested the same ethnic orgins as the taut stretched skin the color and texture of tanned leather.

A lifetime ago—he thought of it in these terms because to recall his childhood and youth was painful and totally futile—it had been easy to detect that he was a half-breed with Latin and European blood coursing through his veins. But during the hardening process of the recent years, when he had spilled a lot of that blood and seen a whole torrent more flowing from the broken bodies of other men, the difference between the features inherited from his Scandinavian mother and his Mexican father had grown more difficult to define. So that now, aged in his mid-thirties, the man's face revealed only that latter portion of his history: it told of pain and heartache: blood-spilling flesh and shattered bones; terror, violence and death.

But it needed more than a first glance to see these things. Just as it needed a closer examination of the man riding the gelding to spot that he was not so relaxed as he looked. In fact, he had been fully alert since first spotting the timber-felled scars in the pine-cloaked valley: his reflexes coiled to spring into instant action. To gallop the gelding; to snatch the Winchester from the boot; to leap from the saddle; to draw the Colt from the holster tied down to his right thigh; to unsheath the cut-throat razor nestling in a leather pouch which slightly bulged his shirt at the back of his neck. Prepared to do any of these things at the merest hint of danger. That he expected and readied himself to meet a threat from the moment he detected the presence of man was a token of the kind of animal instincts which had replaced the human values of which he had been stripped. Such was this lone rider nearing the crest of the rise. The man called Edge.

He reached the top of the slope and reined the gelding to a halt. His narrowed eyes, which had given the clue to his inner tension as they raked the trees on either side of the trail, now focused upon a far larger mark of human presence than any they had so far seen. And one that had not been abandoned. The new section of the valley Edge surveyed was much longer than the one he had just negotiated. Perhaps three miles before the next wave of land with the snowy-peaked mountain ridges visible over the crest. A quarter of the way along, this east-to-west valley was intersected by another which cut across from north to south. A river some hundred feet wide flowed across the intersection and the buildings of a medium-sized town crouched on the eastern bank. A trestle bridge spanned the river, to connect the town with a large lumber mill on the far side. Beyond the mill, which was bounded on one side by the river and a high, wire mesh fence on the others, a trail ran arrow-straight across a vast wasteland of pine stumps and disappeared into the trees which were next in line to be felled.

Although there was not a soul to be seen on the street that ran down to the bridge, or within the bounds of the lumber mill, there were many signs that the town was inhabited. Several horses were tied to hitching rails outside the various business premises. Two dogs slept on the river bank. A half-dozen flatbed wagons with teams in the traces were parked in the shade of the mill. The water wheel at the side of the mill turned lazily. Smoke from cooking fires columned up into the hot, still air from many chimneys.

After Edge had heeled the gelding forward, the town was lost to sight; for this part of the new section of valley had been spared the lumbermen's axes. And he was on level ground for several minutes, still following the disused trail, before he

7

emerged from the tree line and saw the town close up. He could smell the wood smoke from the fires now, strangely refreshing after so long of breathing the sterile scent of pine. He halted the gelding again, lit a cigarette and raked his gaze down the sun-bright street that began fifty yards from where he watched.

It looked a nice, peaceful, clean town. Inevitably in such forest country, all the buildings were constructed of timber. Single story houses standing in neatly fenced gardens at this end. Then, down toward the bridge spanning the river, the business premises which were a mixture of one and two floored buildings. Across the river, and just beginning to cast a shadow toward the town as the sun moved down for its nightly rendezvous with the far end of the valley, the lumber mill thrust upwards to four storeys.

A man who was prone to flights of fancy might have considered the stretching shadow symbolic of a power which the mill maintained over the town. Then, catching the scent of fresh sawdust mingling with the wood smoke, he might have regarded this as strengthening the vaguely menacing atmosphere that clung to the town. The impression augmented by the complete silence that invested the place with a quality that was eerie in its own right. But no such imaginative thoughts struck Edge. It was a lumber town and people either worked with timber or they didn't live here. It was so quiet because the weather was too hot to encourage noisy activity: and it was eating time, to boot.

He read the faded paint lettering on the town marker nailed to a leaning post at the side of the trail and allowed that it spelled out a strange name. But folks were free to call the place where they lived by whatever name they chose. This was a town called Hate.

What interested him more as he urged the gelding forward was another word: painted on a board which jutted out from the front of a two story building close to the far end of the street. It announced: HOTEL. This was not faded like the lettering on the sign. Nothing about the town, except for its marker sign, was faded. The gardens were well-tended and ablaze with colorful flowers in neat beds. Highly-polished windows reflected the sun and painted woodwork gleamed. The water in the trough out front of the livery stable where Edge allowed his horse to drink was as crystal clear as that from a spring. The horses hitched in front of the bank, the law office, the express depot and a row of three stores were in the peak of condition and wore saddles and bridles with the sheen of careful oiling. The mounds at the side of the church were cloaked with well-trimmed grass. The freshly dug grave was a precise rectangle with the soil heaped neatly at the side. Across the street, the lawn fronting the courthouse was as level as a pool table.

Next to the church was the preacher's house, then came the hotel. Above the double-doored entrance was a board proclaiming the name of the place: THE LAST DROP. Edge angled the gelding toward the hitching rail before the entrance and remained in the saddle for a few moments. He sensed watching eyes, and pin-pointed the position of the observer before swinging wearily down to the ground. His feet kicked up the dust of a long, hot summer. From this end of the street the silence

9

of the town was broken by the wet, cool, churning sound of the water wheel turned by the flowing river.

"Hope that sign don't mean this place is about to run out of beer," he drawled, slightly higher than normal conversational level as he hitched the reins of the gelding around the rail.

The door of the preacher's house—like many others he had past on the slow ride along the street—stood open. The interior of the house was in deep shade, but Edge knew somebody was in there, looking out at him. He had not looked at the open doorway since dismounting and now he had his back to it as he reached up and slid the Winchester from the boot.

"If you care to see what is at the other side of the hotel, the significance of the name may strike you as humorous." The voice had a booming quality, although the words were soft spoken. The kind of voice with which preachers are born or acquire with their cloth.

Edge moved across the front of the hotel without turning to look at the man. The street had no sidewalks and his weary feet billowed more dust. An alley separated the hotel from the Corners Bank. Not a wide alley: but broad enough to accommodate a stoutly made platform with steps leading up to it. The ugly framework of a gallows jutted up from one side of the platform. A noose hung down, motionless: so that the rope appeared as rigid as the wood from which it was suspended. There was a lever connected with a weighted trapdoor set into the platform immediately beneath the noose. The whole structure had the quality of permanence and was as well cared for as everything else about the town.

The half-breed turned and recrossed in front of the hotel. The preacher had stepped out of his house now and stood in the lesser shade of the porch roof. He was a small man of sixty or so, with a bulging stomach and fleshy, pink face. Deep lines cut away from the corners of his eyes and mouth and his woeful expression fitted into them precisely. "You see the point of the joke?" he asked, beginning to sweat. He was fully dressed for his duties in black cloth with starched dog collar. A well-used prayer book was clutched in his pudgy hands, resting on his stomach hump.

Edge cracked his lips to show a cold smile that did not reach his eyes. "Does anybody die laughing, reverend?" he asked.

"What do you think?"

"That dying's a serious business." He turned toward the hotel entrance. "For the guys that's doing it."

"Most people think that way," the preacher replied. "Some do not. No point in going inside yet," he hurried on as Edge moved toward the double doorway. "Everybody's over at the courthouse for the trial."

Edge halted and turned around to look across at the neat, white double story building behind the well-trimmed lawn. "Likely to take long?"

"Any time now, stranger. Court convened thirty minutes ago."

Edge backed up to rest his hip against the window sill of the hotel. "Open and shut case, uh?"

"Ezra Hyams is guilty," the preacher answered.

"Of what?"

11

"Spitting in the street."

Edge snapped his head around to search the pink face for a sign of humor. The woeful frown was still carved there. "And the whole town goes to the trial? Hate must be a real fun place to live, reverend."

"It's not the trial so much," the preacher replied, flinching into tenseness. "The rule is that anybody who doesn't attend cannot witness the hanging. Justice must be seen to be done."

The shadows had lengthened to the extent that the looming structure of the lumber mill now cast a great wedge of shade across the river to touch the fringes of the town. There were more sounds now discernible: the droning of flies on the wing, the scrape of hooves as horses scratched impatiently at the dusty street, the distant crying of a waking baby and the low growling of one of the two dogs as they loped past Edge. All this against the background monotony of the churning water wheel. It was still blazingly hot.

"Digging a man's grave before the trial and then hanging him for spitting in the street is justice?" Edge asked wryly.

He didn't care, one way or the other, but conversation was filling the time until the trial was over and someone from the hotel would rent him a room and fix a tub for him.

"Sure is when the spit hits the street just as Mr. Corners is passing by."

It was an odd name: memorable because of its strangeness. Edge asked: "Any kin to Joe Corners?"

The preacher shot a quizzical glance toward Edge, then sighed. "Joe was Mr. Corners' son. He's dead."

12

The half-breed knew it. A bounty-hunter who got greedy and turned to bank robbery. A blown safe door sliced his leg off and a hail of gunfire finished him in a small town in the Dakotas.* It had been winter then and it was pleasant in this heat to recall the biting chill of the air streaming across the frost-cloaked Badlands. But cool thoughts were no substitute for cool water.

"Corners is the big man in Hate, uh?"

Again the preacher became tense at the mention of the town's name. Edge's narrowed eyes spotted the change, then saw the fat old man struggle back to his normal level of composure.

"Mr. Corners runs the mill, the bank, the hotel, the livery and all the stores. He's also the sheriff and the judge."

"That's pretty big," Edge allowed wryly.

A short silence settled between the two men. Another man broke it—with a high-pitched scream of anguish. It sounded distant but in fact came from the courthouse, the stout walls of which had trapped inside the less strident noises of the proceedings. The aggressively-minded dog barked once then returned to his listless rest beneath the water trough. The sun had sunk low enough to pitch the shadow of the mill twenty yards along the street. The heat stayed high.

"Reckon he's guilty," Edge muttered wryly.

The doors at the head of the courthouse steps folded inwards and the judge emerged, untying a cord at his neck to remove a black cape. Beneath this he wore neatly pressed pants and a matching vest unbuttoned to show a crisp white shirt with a silver star pinned to the left breast pocket.

* *See Edge: Bloody Summer.*

13

He was a big man in good condition, his torso tapering down from massive shoulders to an almost slim waist. He had long legs. His face showed more than fifty years of living, most of them hard. A high forehead under close-cropped, silver grey hair; brooding brown eyes set deep and wide; full mouth above a jutting jawline; a nose beaten out of shape so that he hung on the verge of handsomeness; a deeply tanned complexion pitted by an ancient illness and scarred by the ruts of time. His movements were lithe and free-flowing. He exuded an aura of powerful self-assurance.

"That's Mr. Corners," the preacher whispered, in the kind of tone he might use to announce the second coming.

The man who owned the town started down the steps. At the top he was smiling but by the time his highly-polished boots were on the cement pathway which divided the lawn in two his expression had altered to a heavy frown. He stared fixedly at Edge, leaving no doubt about the cause of his displeasure.

"He just rode in, Mr. Corners!" the preacher called hurriedly. Apologetically.

More people emerged from the courthouse. A ruggedly built youngster in his early twenties wearing a gunbelt and hat of his own and carrying a higher quality set of the same gear. He handed them to Corners and as the former judge now sheriff exchanged the cape for the belt and hat, the man scheduled to be hanged came out into the sunlight. He was weak-looking, with a bald head and a mask of anguish twisting his face. He wore a storekeeper's apron. Quaking with terror, he looked ready to collapse, but two men supported him.

14

Like the youngster who took care of Corners' gear and three other men, they wore deputy's badges. The citizens of Hate who had no power in the town filed out of the courthouse in ranks of two, in procession behind Corners as he led the way across the street. The men, women and children wore no badges. They did wear expressions of meek sadness.

Halfway to the mouth of the alley, Corners finished buckling on his gunbelt with just the single holster on the right hip. He halted abruptly and fixed Edge with another dark-eyed stare.

"Man's allowed to carry sidearms but not rifles inside town limits, mister," he pronounced. His voice matched his physique: powerful. "And we like folks to be clean."

He had a great many shining examples in back of him. Apart from the sweat on their faces, every man, woman and child appeared to have stepped straight from a tub into their Sunday-best clothes. The vast majority of the upwards of thirty men wore holstered revolvers. Edge's pants and shirt were caked with dirt held on the fabric by old sweat. His low-crowned hat had been changed from black to grey by the dust of travel. A forty-eight our growth of bristle sprouted from the dirt-grimed skin of his face. The Winchester was held easily in his left hand, pointing at the ground.

"Happy to get separated from the dirt, sheriff," he replied evenly, aware of the massed stare focused upon him. "Just as soon as somebody's ready to fill a tub for me. Stow the rifle soon as I reckon I won't need it."

There was no actual noise from the group of watchers. But the half-breed sensed a great intake of breath, which was held for the brittle silence while Corners glowered at Edge.

"Nobody's fired a gun in Corners for five years, mister," the man of many parts said gravely. "Obey the town ordinances and you've got nothing to fear."

"Obliged for the information," Edge replied, noting that the town had a new name different from the one on the sagging marker sign. "Real anxious to abide by the rule about being clean. So if you'd just get on with the lynching."

This time the crowd did give vent to its shock. A series of gasps quivered in the hot air. The redness of anger spread beneath Corners' tan. His deputies toughened their expressions. The condemned Ezra Hyams emitted a mournful groan.

"This is a legal execution carried out under due process of law," Corners intoned.

Edge sighed. "Okay, sheriff. Call it whatever the hell you like. Hate's your town."

The sound of massed shock was loud enough to mask the churning water wheel for a fleeting moment. But not the slap of flesh on leather and the metallic click as four of the deputies drew their revolvers and cocked them simultaneously. The two supporting Hyams had to be content with tightening their grip on the doomed man. He groaned again. Corners quivered with rage, then struggled to contain it. His powerful voice sounded strained.

A much colder anger glinted in the blue slits of Edge's eyes. It was firmly in control as he raked his stare over the faces of the men aiming guns at him. Each of the deputies was hard and capable and wore the indefinable stamp of those who are prepared to kill. But each of them betrayed a tremor

16

of naked fear as he returned the stare of the half-breed. For each recognized that he faced a man far more experienced in the way of sudden death than he was. Experienced and adept: for this man was not hampered by the reflex-slowing influence of fear.

"I got this allergy toward pointing guns, sheriff," Edge said in quiet-voiced earnestness. "Tell your boys to either blast me or holster those Colts real quick."

"So you came in on the old east trail and the sign's still there," Corners said levelly, as if he had not heard the half-breed's comment. "I hanged the man who put up that sign. And warned that anyone who referred to the town as anything except Corners would get the same treatment."

"What about those guns?" Edge said in the soft-toned voice.

Corners ignored it again. "But you're a stranger and I guess the preacher man didn't give you the word. So I'll just put you on probation for the time you're in town. Break that probation in any way and I'll put you under arrest."

As Corners was announcing his intention, Edge moved his hip off the sill and stood erect with his back to the window. The Winchester stayed pointing at the ground, but it was no longer held in a loose grip. Like every other muscle in his lean body, those in the half-breed's hand were knotted tight. The deputies sensed a change in Edge but could see nothing positive. Although he had moved slightly, his stance continued to look loose limbed and relaxed. He appeared totally incapable of backing up the menace of his expression and soft-spoken words.

17

"The guns, Corners," Edge urged, paying as scant attention to the sheriff's words as the man had paid to his. He sensed a kind of breathless excitement emanating from the preacher but did not look toward him.

"I give my men their orders in my own good time mister," Corners growled.

"It ran out," Edge replied, and launched into violent action.

At one instant he was lounging in his pretence of relaxation. The next he had flung himself into a backward leap. He powered himself clear of the ground tucked his chin hard down against his chest and crashed his shoulders into the window. The window comprised a dozen small panes held into the main frame by slender cross frames. Wood snapped and glass shattered under the impact of his lunging weight. He arched his body over the jagged pinnacles of broken glass and thudded hard to the floor inside the hotel. The fallen debris crunched and splintered under him as he rolled on to his belly and thrust up into a crouch, whirling to peer out of the window along the barrel of the Winchester. He drew a bead on the glinting silver star pinned over Corners' heart. The action scraped.

The whole incident had taken no more than three seconds. Time enough for the crowd to scatter and the deputies to fire. But nobody had moved so much as a trigger finger. Just the odd facial muscle so that a few of the townspeople arrayed behind the lawmen betrayed faint smiles.

"Either they put those irons where they belong or that star gets blasted out through your back,"

Edge announced. "I think—" the deputy holding the cape began.

"I *know* he means it," Corners cut in, and now he was pallid under the tan. From a higher plane of rage rather than fear. "Put the guns away men."

The violent exertion had erupted sweat from every pore in Edge's body. But the eye behind the Winchester's back-sight was cracked too narrow to admit the salty beads dripping from his forehead.

"Hey, mister!" Ezra Hyams shouted, his tone akin to delight. "Now you got the drop on 'em, make 'em let me go."

The silent mood of some of the people in the crowd changed from just visible glee to ardent hope. Edge stifled it.

"Everyone's got problems feller," he answered. "I just take care of my own."

He was immediately an object of contempt in the eyes of the townspeople. The deputies showed him hate. Corners was suddenly like a man eyeing a piece of prime property he considered buying as he looked at Edge through the shattered window.

"You just broke probation, mister," he accused without rancor.

Edge stood up, presenting a much bigger target through the jagged glass opening. The aim of the rifle was negligent, from the hip. But everyone was now fully aware of his speed. "All I broke was a window," he replied quietly. "Another gun points at me in this town and it'll be the guy holding it that gets smashed up. You want to string him up now, so I can get a bath?"

"Thanks one hell of a lot, you bastard!" Ezra Hyams screamed, and sagged between his captors his body wracked with sobs.

"Spitting *and* using bad language," Edge mocked as Corners led the procession forward. "You were born to hang, feller."

The preacher crossed in front of the broken window, clutching his prayer book more firmly to his bulbous stomach and fixing a solemn expression on his pink features. Edge leaned out through the glinting shards still slotted into the main frame and saw the townspeople form into orderly rows at the mouth of the alley. All were gazing with hypnotic fascination toward the gallows. Against the churning of the water wheel there was now just the deep-throated sobbing of the condemned man. Then the hollow thud of footfalls on the steps and platform. A piercing scream cut through the stifling air. It ended abruptly with the crack of a hand on flesh. Flies droned and there was a pained yelp as one of the dogs opened his mouth too wide for a yawn. The preacher began to intone the Lord's Prayer into the quietness of the late afternoon.

"May God have mercy on your soul," he concluded.

Hyams screamed for a final time. The release lever creaked. The trap door opened with a crack. Hyams' neck broke with a muffled snap. The audience of townspeople did not make a sound until they turned away from the gruesome sight of the limply suspended body. And then there was just the shuffling of their feet dragging through the dust. A gamut of expressions from horror to abject misery was carved upon their faces. A tall, thin old man shuffled toward the hotel entrance. He was trailed by another, half his age who looked enough like him to be his son. Both halted at the doorway and looked balefully along the hotel frontage at Edge leaning out of the window.

"It's disgusting," the old man muttered, his bloodless lips trembling. "They hang some poor wretch and make us line up to look at it. Like it's some kind of entertainment we're supposed to enjoy."

His son glanced around nervously, as if fearful the words would be overheard.

"Seems like it was a lousy show," Edge replied wryly. "Only the one guy had a swinging time."

CHAPTER TWO

SINCE Edge was the only guest, he was offered the pick of the rooms in The Last Drop Hotel. Because the first floor of the place was completely taken up by a saloon, restaurant and living quarters for the old man and his son, all the rented accommodation was on the second floor. The half-breed selected a room at the front at the far end of the hallway. It had a window overlooking the street and no other way in but through the door—which had a lock that worked. The room was at the opposite end of the building from the saloon on the floor below, but this was not a consideration in choosing it. For, even at the best of times, the town called Hate did not seem to be the kind of community in which rowdiness was tolerated.

The men who ran the hotel were named Mc-Nally. Cyrus was the old man and his son was Billy. Cyrus had accepted two dollars as advance payment for one night's room rent. It was Billy who lugged a tin tub into the room and made a half dozen trips down and up the stairs with a pitcher to fill it with water from the pump out back. Edge gave him a dollar and a half and began to unbutton his shirt.

"Gee that's a big tip, mister," Billy exclaimed, his weak eyes gleaming with delight.

The man's natural ugliness was made more so by his emaciation. Fate had been even more unkind and given him a simple mind.

22

Edge shook his head. "Fifty cents for your trouble. Dollar for the liveryman to take care of my horse and gear for the night." He looked hard at Billy. "Can you do that?"

The man carefully segregated the fifty cents from the dollar in separate pockets, his happiness unimpaired. "Gee, mister. I can't remember the last time I was give any money."

"Just remember to fix up my horse," Edge told him, and nodded toward the door.

The man went out, still wearing his broad grin and Edge locked the door behind him. Then he crossed to the window and saw that the street was empty in the fading light as afternoon closed with evening. All the horses except his own were gone. The dogs rose from under the trough, stretched and began to prowl, sniffing at lingering smells with the boredom of familiarity. The only signs of human activity were out at the lumber mill on the far side of the river. Four men—to distant to be recognizable—were unharnessing the teams from the wagons. Then a movement below captured the half-breed's attention and he snapped his head around, hooded eyes raking the street. But it was only Billy McNally unhitching the gelding to lead him along to the livery stable.

Edge did not grin at his whiplash response to what turned out to be the innocent action of a simpleton. Rather, he accepted it as the norm and was impassively satisfied. For there was always the danger that, in the period of anti-climax following an explosion of violent action, a man's reflexes might be dulled. And if Edge was to stay alive he could not afford the luxury of dropping his guard for even a moment. Thus, as he stripped off his travel-

23

stained topclothes and then peeled the red under-
wear from his sweat-tacky body, the Winchester
was close at hand, resting across the bed. His lithe
muscular body was just a shade lighter than his
face: except for the puckered, livid scar tissue of
healed bullet wounds at his left shoulder and thigh
and right hip. These were the visible marks left
upon him by that metamorphic period in his life
when he learned how to kill without compunc-
tion.*

As he lowered himself gratefully into the tepid
water his lean features betrayed nothing of the
pleasure he experienced: and this constantly indif-
ferent attitude to outside influences had also been
a legacy of those blood-drenched days, weeks,
months and years which forged him from a sensitive youth into a machine-like man. And almost everything that had happened to him during the in-
tervening years had served to harden him in the
mould that fate had shaped for him.

Edge raised his naked body from the water and
soaped the firm, rippling flesh. No, not *almost* everything. *Everything*. For even his marriage to Elizabeth and the true happiness it brought him was all
a part of life's grand plan to cause him pain and
suffering. A vicious trick that offered him hope and
then shattered it with the most tragic blow he had
ever been struck.*

He sat down in the tub again and rinsed off the
lather, turning the water from grey to black. Then
he soaped his face and drew the razor from its
pouch, still held at the back of his neck by the

* *See—the Civil War books beginning with Edge: Killer's
Breed.*
* *See Edge: Sioux Uprising.*

24

leather thong strung with beads. He shaved quickly with long strokes that rasped off the bristles and
when he was finished he stepped from the tub and
toweled himself. It was murky in the room now, as
the red glow of sunset beyond the window changed
to the darkening shade of twilight. He shook the
dust from his clothes and dressed. With the advance of evening the temperature had fallen a little, but the air had become humid and the mild ex-
ertions of drying himself, shaking his clothes and
then putting them on opened his pores again.

Sticky, but clean, he left the room carrying the
Winchester and not locking the door for there was
nothing on the other side to steal. A series of regular banging sounds reached toward him as he
moved along the hallway and the noise swelled as
he started down the stairs. The stairway canted
across the rear wall of the saloon. The bar counter
ran the length of a side wall with a scattering of tables and chairs spread in front of it. Open double
doors in the opposite wall gave on to the restaurant.

It was from the saloon that the banging came as
Cyrus McNally hammered boards into position
over the broken window. It was the big room's
only window and the doors had been wedged open
to allow in a trickle of humid air. Not light, for the
saloon was well provided for by kerosene lamps
hung from ceiling and walls. The pallid, painfully
thin old man completed the chore with a sigh and
shuffled across toward the bar counter as Edge stepped down into the saloon. McNally went through a
gap at the far end of the counter and discarded the
hammer and spare nails on his shuffling journey to

where Edge stood with a foot hooked over the brass rail.

"Whisky, sir?" the old man croaked, his lips trembling and his watery eyes apprehensive.

"I tried that and it didn't work," Edge replied evenly. "Beer."

The pump was a few feet along the counter and McNally's hands shook as he worked the lever and held the glass beneath the pipe. His eyes flicked away from what he was doing to Edge, and back again. The half-breed was aware of the man's nervousness but ignored it for a few moments as he recalled the blurred days and nights when he had sought solace for the loss of Elizabeth by trying to heal the emotional wound with alcohol. The decision to attempt such a solution had been completely alien to his nature. But his act of aiding—rather than killing—a young couple who had cheated him to raise the money to get married had been even more out of character.*

He had been lucky. For once, fate had been benevolent. He had carried his recollections of the soon-to-be-married couple into a small town in the heart of Wyoming Territory. A town where there was no hint of trouble to trigger the latent violence that lurked in every fiber of his being. In that town, haunted by thoughts of the couple, his mind thrust forward memories of how Elizabeth had lived and died: memories he had been fooled into believing were as irrecoverably buried as her body. But they were not buried, so he had attempted to drown them.

After it was over, they told him he had spent

* See Edge: The Biggest Bounty.

eight days in the twilight realm of drunkenness where the difference between waking and sleeping was marked by the slumped or upright posture of a man's body. Eight days during which any of the countless enemies he had made could have killed him as if he were a defenseless baby.

"Your drink, sir," the old man said as he set down the foaming glass in front of Edge. "Mark it on your bill?"

"Obliged, but I pay as I go" the half-breed replied absently dropping a handful of coins on the counter top.

And when the eight day drunk was over and Edge started the long, aimless ride that had brought him to Hate, he could feel content with only one aspect of the wasted days. Never again would he leave himself vulnerable in such a way— or in any other way. Elizabeth? Whisky had solved nothing in relation to curing the hurt of losing her which was still imbedded deep inside of him. The ache was duller, maybe. But that was due to the passage of time. When a longer time had passed, the anguish would lessen even more. It had worked for him before.

"Pardon me, sir?"

Edge was sipping the beer. It was fresh and cool from the cask stored in the basement. "Yeah?"

"You give my boy some money." The old man blurted out the words fast, as if afraid of their effect and hopeful that speed would lessen it.

"I ain't all bad," Edge replied, cracking his lips in a grin that showed his even teeth very white against his dark complexion.

"No offense but . . ." The old man took a hand from his vest pocket and dropped a half dollar

27

piece on the pile of change. He took ten cents back from the money, attention concentrated upon what he was dong so that he did not have to meet the half-breed's quizzical gaze

"For the beer," McNally went on as footfalls sounded on the threshold of the saloon. He leaned to the side to look around Edge and smiled, glad to have another customer. "Evening, reverend."

"When somebody gives me money, I'm not offended" Edge said recalling the younger McNally's joy at receiving the tip. "But I guess Billy's feeling pretty sore."

The preacher pressed his prominent belly against the bar six feet to Edge's left. He still wore his clerical garb but had left the prayer book at home. McNally set down a shot glass in front of his new customer and filled it to the brim with whisky. He left the bottle.

"Something I should have told you about Billy" McNally said when he had finished the serving chore.

"That he was at the end of the line when they handed out minds," Edge suggested.

"That," McNally allowed hurriedly. "But I guess a man can figure that for himself. Just by talking to Billy for a minute. No, I should have warned you about giving him money. See, soon as he gets any—don't matter how little it is—he sets off walking to another town. Even if it's just a couple of pennies, he reckons it for a stake. Got no money sense, like. Just knows he needs a stake to start living someplace else."

Edge finished his beer. "If he wants to do that, he ain't so simple as he looks," he said wryly nodding to the glass to order another beer.

McNally hurried to get the order, less apprehensive of approaching Edge now that the explanation had been accepted so calmly. He had lived a long life, but he had no wish to have it foreshortened by this tall stranger who seemed to emanate an aura of latent violence from the center of his coldly calm being.

"This isn't such a bad town if you live by the rules," the preacher said conversationally as fresh beer gushed into the glass.

Edge turned slightly, to lean a hip against the bar, fixing a level gaze upon the pink face above the starched white collar. "About those rules?" he said quietly.

The preacher blinked, obviously regretting the impulse to speak with Edge. "Yes?"

"Hi, Mr. NcNally; preacher." This from a woman who strolled into the saloon, her voice bright and her walk bouncy.

"Evening, Miss Dorrie" McNally responded to the greeting.

Edge glanced at the woman, beginning his cursory examination at the polished toes of her black riding boots and finishing it at the crown of her jet black hair. In between he saw the promise of long legs hidden by the boots and a green skirt that fell to just above her ankles: a heavy-breasted narrow-waisted torso tightly encased in a white blouse; and a pretty, snub-nosed, blue-eyed full-mouth face. When his narrowed eyes met her wide ones Edge displayed blank indifference. The woman's expression conveyed cool appraisal.

Edge looked back at the preacher and some of the bounce went out of Dorrie's deportment as she swayed to a table and sat down. A look akin to a glower of rejection marred her prettiness.

"A bottle of imported champagne Mr. McNally," she called and her change of mood was also detectable in her voice.

"Like McNally could have told me about his boy," Edge said to the preacher.

The fat man took the rest of his drink at a swallow and poured another. The bartender set down the beer and moved quickly to supply the woman's order.

"You could have told me a couple of things," the half-breed continued in the same easy tone. He used his knee to nudge the Winchester resting against the bar front. "Like the rule about not letting Corners' sensitive eyes see one of these. And about Hate being a dirty word in this town."

The pink of the preacher's complexion had become concentrated into small red patches at the centers of his cheeks.

"Would it have made any difference to a man like you?" the woman asked, her tone taunting.

Edge looked at her again. For a little longer this time. He fixed her age somewhere in the late twenties. She had grown up with a great deal of arrogance and a lot of style. She was in the man's world of a saloon and yet appeared neither out of place not whorishly in her element as she watched the nervous McNally work loose the cork from the champagne bottle.

"Who asked you to butt in?" the half-breed rasped.

She flinched at the tone, but maintained the steady challenge in her wide eyes. "You've talked the preacher man into a bad scare, mister," she replied as the cork exploded and champagne gushed. She raised the glass for McNally to fill it. "This is a healthy town. People grow real old before they die. Unless they're stupid enough to cross Luke Corners and he's in a hanging mood."

A group of four men entered the saloon and hesitated sensing the nervousness of McNally and the preacher; the brittle tension between the half-breed and the woman. But then they decided they were committed and they moved up to the bar counter—as far away from Edge as they could get. McNally went to attend to their needs as fast as his ancient legs would carry him.

"So?" Edge asked, addressing the preacher.

The man flapped open his mouth to reply, but the words wouldn't come. There was a lot of sweat coursing down his face and some droplets splashed from his upper to his lower lip. His tongue darted out to lick away the salty moisture.

"A real bad scare," Edge allowed, swinging his gaze back toward the woman.

Dorrie liked to be proved right and smiled her pleasure as she sipped champagne. "Uncle Luke doesn't pay for preaching, mister. He says good deeds are better than good words. And he's generous when it comes to keeping the smell of the dead out of this town. The preacher boxes them as well as burying them. And, like I said, it's a long time between natural deaths."

As Edge turned his slitted eyes back toward the preacher, the man reached for his shot glass, and knocked it over with a trembling hand. Attention was riveted upon Edge. Every man in the saloon could recall how the half-breed had exploded from apparent casual repose into violent action.

"Explains why you almost burst your breeches with excitement when the Corners' muscle pulled out the guns," Edge said evenly.

The preacher gulped, and freed his vocal chords. "Someone has to bury the dead," he croaked.

"Sure," Edge replied trying his new beer. He showed his teeth in the cold grin that did not reach his eyes. "Natural progression I guess. Set them up to get hung, cut them down and bury them. Quite an undertaking."

"I didn't . . . ." the preacher began as two more customers came into the saloon. Then he decided not to push his luck with excuses. He delved under his cassock, pulled out a bill and slapped it on the bar: turned, and avoiding a clash of eyes with anybody in the saloon, hurried to the doorway and went out.

There were a few moments of silence in the over-heated kerosene and whisky-fetid atmosphere of the big room. Then the boots of the newcomers scuffed against the floorboards, the men heading for the table where Dorrie sat.

"Thanks for not causing no trouble, sir," McNally said in a hushed whisper.

But his voice carried to the table where the two men were about to sit down.

"Ain't insulting a lady trouble Mr. McNally?" Dorrie demanded.

Edge was looking into the face of the old bartender. He saw the expression of heartfelt relief wiped away by the familiar look of apprehension.

"That drifter insulted you?" a man asked.

Edge turned to rest his back against the bar. His left hand hung close to the muzzle of the leaning Winchester. His right was hooked loosely around

32

the holster tied down to his right thigh. His hooded eyes shifted from one of the men at the table to the other. The lamplight reflected on their tin stars. The deputy with the black hair was the one who had looked after Corners' hat and gun during the trial. The blond lawman was one of those who had held Ezra Hyams captive. It was he who had spoken the challenging words, apparently after brushing his lips across the cheek of the suddenly incensed woman. Rage flickered in his dark eyes, on the point of flaring.

"What happened?" he demanded, staring at Edge but addressing the question to Dorrie.

Edge spoke into the short, tense silence. "Same as now, feller."

"What the hell is that supposed to mean?" the deputy snarled.

Everyone was sweating. The fire of his anger made his face more sheened than any other. He was sitting very erect in the chair, muscles tensed to spring him out of it.

"He told me to butt out, George," Dorrie supplied huffily. "As soon as I opened my mouth. Is that anyway to talk to a lady?"

"No way," Edge agreed. "My mistake, Miss Dorrie."

Confusion showed in the faces of the two lawmen and the woman. Edge heard a ripple of scornful sounds from the throats of the four men at the end of the bar.

"I should think so!" the woman murmured with a triumphant smile.

"Thing is," Edge continued. "I didn't know you were a lady. Figured you for a latrine digger, what with the stink of all that crap you stir."

33

George thrust upright from his chair and it fell backwards. The sound as it hit the floor cut across a series of gasps.

"Don't draw on him, George!" the second deputy yelled, his fearful gaze glued to the tall form of the half-breed.

"Shut up, Ernie!" George snarled but halted the movement of his hand toward his gun. "Ain't no bastard goin' to get away with smart-talkin' my girl."

Edge waited impassively, hooded eyes fastened upon George. But on the periphery of his vision he could see the worried Ernie and the enraged Dorrie.

"I'm gonna take out my iron and drop it on the floor," George said, softly and slowly, to puncture the pause. "Then if you don't blast me I'm gonna beat the hell out of you."

Dorrie's anger was waft away by a rising excitement.

"Outside please, Mr. Bradbury!" McNally pleaded. "You know Mr. Corners holds me responsible for damage."

"I'll pay for the breakages," George Bradbury replied, continuing to hold Edge's level stare as he slowly eased the gun from the holster. He held the butt lightly between thumb and forefinger and as soon as the barrel was clear, he released his grip. The Colt fell heavily and bounced once.

"His estate will pay," Edge said, moving away from the bar as a new group of customers came in through the doorway. He went to the side slightly, so that he could glance at the soloon entrance without losing sight of Bradbury. Six men. No deputies. They looked bewildered at the set up which greet-

34

ed them, but then recognized the two men who were the center of the riveted interest. They showed half-concealed pleasure as they moved toward the bar in a wide half circle, staying clear of the closing forms of Bradbury and Edge. "Watch the Winchester for me, Cyrus," the half-breed added. "Rifle must be a valuable piece of property in Hate."

His use of the forbidden name created no stir now since there was already a good reason for the fight.

As Edge had moved to the side, so had Bradbury, shuffling away from the table where his fellow-deputy still sat beside the excited woman. Dorrie was chewing at her nails. Edge halted the circling motion long before he put his back toward Ernie. He stopped in a position from which he could center his attention on Bradbury but also see the couple at the table, the doorway and the men at the bar. He saw McNally's skinny arm snake over the counter and hoist up the Winchester. The rifle disappeared from sight.

"Ain't fair!" Ernie said sharply. "George ain't armed. You've got a gun in that holster, mister."

"Same as you," Edge answered.

"I ain't involved."

"Keep it that way and live longer," the half-breed had time to reply before Bradbury lunged at him.

He was more than two inches shorter than Edge's six-three but looked to weigh about the same. But he came nowhere close to matching the half-breed for agility. He charged across the six feet of floor space, chin tucked down against his broad chest, left fist raised in a guard attitude and right

35

arm thrust out in front of him. The bunched fist at the end of the leading arm looked big and hard. Edge feigned to the left then leaned suddenly to the right. Bradbury veered to the first direction but didn't have the time to correct his mistake.

As his attacker stopped in his tracks with a grunt and starting to swing a roundhouse, Edge folded his long body into a crouch. He clasped both hands into a single fist and launched them forward. His shoulders were on a level with Bradbury's stomach as the deputy turned. Edge aimed the two-handed punch lower and smashed his clasped knuckles into the bulge of the man's crotch. Bradbury screamed and staggered back, doubling his body and dropping both hands to clutch at the source of his agony.

Edge sprang forward from his crouch, hands still clasped together. The locked fingers dropped over Bradbury's head and tangled in his hair. When Edge snapped up his arms, Bradbury was forced to straighten. His face was a mask of agony: a thousand beads of sweat standing out against the deathly white of his skin. The weak end of the scream trailed from his gaping mouth. Edge stared coldly into the twisted features: and from the corner of his slitted eyes he saw beyond them. To the frightened Ernie, the fascinated Dorrie, and the horrified preacher framed in the doorway. The preacher ducked out of sight.

The half-breed jerked Bradbury's head down—and brought up his knee. The two collided with a sickening crunch of bone against bone. Edge felt dampness on his pants leg and when he released the suddenly limp and silent Bradbury, he saw the blood stain. The deputy fell hard on to the base of his spine and sprawled backwards, displaying his face to the audience. The entire lower half of his features was coated with slick, shiny blood. His ragged breathing bubbled fresh ooze from the flattened wreckage of his smashed nose.

"Reckon the stink of you won't bother your boyfriend," Edge told the woman.

Dorrie's high excitement nose-dived into a fit of rage as she dragged her wide eyes away from the mutilated face of Bradbury to glare at Edge. "You ain't won yet, mister!" she snarled.

She grabbed the bottle of champagne, leaned forward and shook it violently with her thumb over the top. Edge sidled back to his former position at the bar. Nobody watched him. All eyes were on the woman as she directed the neck of the bottle toward Bradbury and removed her thumb. A white gush of foam jetted into the face of the deputy and sprayed away, tinted red by the blood. Bradbury shook his head and groaned as he tried to dodge the vicious pounding of the wine against a new seat of agony.

"Get up you yellow rat!" Dorrie screamed as the bottle was emptied. "A bum insults me and you take a dive as soon as he touches you."

"Dorrie, he's had enough!" Ernie implored, staring in horror at Bradbury as the injured man rolled over on to his stomach.

"Shut your mouth, Bucher!" the woman ranted. "Or go get the bum yourself."

Ernie Bucher looked fearfully across at Edge. The half-breed was leaning against the bar, drinking his beer: left-handed, so that his right could caress the holster with long, brown-skinned fingers.

37

The deputy clamped his lips tightly together and pressed himself hard against the back of his chair.

"Come on get up!" Dorrie shrieked.

Bradbury forced himself on to all fours and rested.

"Not only smells like one," Edge muttered into the hot silence punctuated by the deputy's pained breathing. "Sounds like a latrine digger, too."

"You hear that, you yellow rat?" Dorrie taunted Bradbury.

The man pushed up with his hands and held a kneeling position for long moments, raking his agony-misted eyes around the faces of the men at the bar. His vision cleared and his gaze zeroed in on Edge. With agonizing slowness, he extricated a foot from under him, stayed kneeling on one leg for a moment, then pushed himself upright. The pain in his crotch would not allow him to stand fully erect and he swayed, leaning forward from the waist.

"He can't take any more, mister!" Bucher implored.

"Go get that bum, George!" Dorrie yelled.

Now that the worst of the blood had been washed from his face Bradbury's nose could be seen as a misshapen pulp with the white of bone and gristle showing amid the ghastly redness. He lumbered forward, feet dragging and arms hanging limp.

"She's making a monkey out of you," Edge called softly.

Just as he had sensed the high excitement of the preacher out on the street in the afternoon sun, so now Edge felt the anticipation generated by the men at the far end of the bar. Men who sensed he was being pushed too far: that asked to finish the

38

fight for a second time, he would leave no opportunity for another comeback. Men who smelt death in the stiflingly humid air of the saloon.

"Slaughter him, George!"

The woman's words were like a physical force slamming into Bradbury's back. The deputy planted his feet firmly on the floor and leaned forward hard, bringing up his arms. The hands were not even clenched into fists. Edge released the glass and it crashed to the bar-rail, shattering and splashing beer across the floor. His boots crunched the shards into sparkling dust as he stepped sideways. Bradbury fell past him, scrabbling up his hands to clutch at the bar counter. Edge's right hand moved as a blur streaking upwards then powering down. The heel of the hand chopped into the hirsute flesh just above Bradbury's shirt collar.

The speed of the man's fall was increased fourfold and his throat smashed into the angle of the bar top and front with the spatter of burst flesh and the crack of fractured bone. Utter silence accompanied the slide of Bradbury's body to the floor. When he was motionless blood oozed from the split skin of his throat. His head lolled at a grotesque angle.

Footfalls sounded on the other side of the bar and Edge looked up to see Billy McNally coming through a doorway. The simple face wore a creased frown as he leaned over to look down at the crumpled body of Bradbury.

"That one always was lookin' for trouble, Mr. Edge," the mentally retarded man said, nodding knowledgeably.

"Then I guess he had to win either way," Edge

39

muttered, stretching out a hand. The elder Mc-Nally pushed the Winchester toward the half-breed. "He either married it or got it in the neck from me."

CHAPTER THREE

"GEORGE!" Dorrie screamed, lunging from her chair and racing across the room. She halted abruptly to stare down in gaping horror at the unmoving, grotesquely postured form of Bradbury.

"He ain't listening," Edge said. "Should have done that while he was still alive."

"I didn't mean for this to happen," the woman moaned, and looked up into the moon face of Billy McNally and the nervousness of his father; then toward the tense expressions shown by the audience of men at the end of the bar. "I didn't mean for anyone to get killed!"

Her voice rose and she whirled around to face Edge her blue eyes blazing against the paleness of her blemish-free complexion. Suddenly, she flung up her hands, fists clenched. Hoofbeats clattered against the street outside. Dorrie lunged at Edge.

The half-breed pushed the Winchester toward the woman, sideways on, to form a bar against her plunging arms. A moment of silence in the sticky heat of the saloon was ended by the unmistakable click of a revolver being cocked. Dorrie gave a cry of pain as her forearms crashed against the rifle. Edge remained facing her, but his ice blue eyes swivelled along their hairline slits. He saw Bucher half raised from his chair, in process of snapping his ready-cocked Colt from its holster.

Edge drew, flicked his wrist to aim in the gap between his own and the woman's body, and fired. The shot was meant to kill, but the deputy lunged upright from his chair at the moment he levelled the revolver. His finger was already squeezing the trigger when the bullet from Edge's Colt burrowed into the flesh of his thigh. The impact of the lead turned him a fraction before he started to topple. His own gun cracked.

"It's Mr. Corners!" Billy shouted.

Dorrie screamed and Edge felt the warm wetness of blood splash across his cheek. Bucher groaned and crashed over a table and on to the floor. Luke Corners ducked his head and rode a white mare into the saloon. He was carrying a double-barreled shotgun.

Edge's glinting eyes changed the direction and focus of their stare to look at Dorrie. Both her arms were hanging over the bar of the Winchester and her chin was hooked on to the clenched fist with which Edge gripped the rifle. Her eyes were screwed tight shut and a curtain of running blood masked the lower part of her right cheek. It issued from a deep furrow that cut across the flesh from under her hair to her upper lip. She was concious, but draping all her weight on to the powerfully held gun.

"Dorrie!" Corners roared. "What happened to you."

He had halted his snorting mount on the threshold and completed a rapid, glowering appraisal of the scene before him. Now, as his eyes were captured by the mutilating wound in the woman's face, concern and quivering rage did battle across his ill-used countenance. Hot silence followed the demand for information.

"Guy with the bum leg shot her" Edge replied easily.

Bucher had struggled into a sitting posture, using both hands to try to stem the gush of blood from his thigh wound. "I meant to blast the drifter, Mr. Corners!" he pleaded through teeth clenched against the pain. "Bastard plugged me."

Corners' shifted his gaze from the drunkenly-leaning woman to the pain-wracked Bucher, then settled on Edge.

"Mr. Edge shot in self defense!" Billy yelled, resolutely holding his position as his father scuttled out of the line of fire.

Corners released his hold on the reins and tilted up the shotgun, gripping it in both hands. Edge, his hooded-eyed, thin-lipped face set in an expression of rock-like impassiveness stepped backwards and turned his body slightly making sure the massive man on the white horse could see the pointing Colt. Without the Winchester to support her, Dorrie fell hard to her knees. She yelled in pain and toppled forward to drape her body across the corpse of Bradbury. Holding on to consciousness, she struggled to rise. But pain and shock had drained her strength and her scrabbling hands slithered in the mixture of her own and the dead man's blood.

"There's been nothing but trouble in this town since you got here!" Corners snarled, careful not to aim the ugly twin muzzles of the shotgun at Edge: canting the gun so that it pointed at the floor a few feet in front of the half-breed.

Edge cracked his lips into a frozen grin. He thrust the Winchester gently across in front of his legs to nudge the struggling Dorrie in the shoulder.

"One of those days, I guess," he drawled. "Just one lousy thing on top of another."

The sardonic comment fed fresh fuel to the fire of Corners' rage and he snatched his glaring gaze away from the calmly detached features of Edge. He stared into the faces of the audience of men at the end of the bar and spotted massed scorn for his frustration in the instant before they cowered away from his rage.

Every watching eye saw the unique sight of the powerful Luke Corners facing up to the defeat which would be marked by inaction. But the big man on the horse refused to surrender as more hoofbeats sounded on the street.

"You blasted my only kin, Bucher!" he roared, swinging the shotgun around and raising it to thud the stock into his shoulder.

"Mr. Corners!" the helpless deputy shrieked, struggling pathetically to get to his feet. "I was—"

Corners squeezed both triggers at once. Bucher had half-risen, hauling himself up by a two-handed grip on the table. The double load of shot went high as the gun bucked. But not high enough. The lower sections of the scatter gouged into Bucher at eye level and went deep, tearing loose flesh and shattering bone. The man died instantly, smashing back to the floor as a great stream of blood, bone, gristle and pulpy brain matter gushed from the jagged hole in his skull.

"Holy cow what a way to go!" Billy yelled gleefully.

"Mind blowing," Edge muttered as Dorrie made it back up to her knees.

Corners' four surviving deputies raced their horses up to the front of the hotel and leapt from

44

their saddles. They ran into the saloon with revolvers drawn, two on each side of the mounted man. They pulled up short, their tough exteriors concealing every other emotion except surprise as they raked their hard-eyed stares over the blood-stained saloon. Then they glanced up at Corners for an order.

The big man turned in the saddle and thrust the still-smoking shotgun into a specially made boot. He glanced first at the knot of men who formed the audience for the slaughter and gave a grunt of satisfaction when he saw the fear they displayed through their horror.

"Keep the drifter covered," he instructed, his voice pitched at a normal level again. "I'm going to get my niece."

He started to dismount as Dorrie hooked blood-dripping hands over the tóp of the bar and hauled herself upright.

"Don't you trust him, Mr. Edge!" Billy warned.

"Billy!" his father cried.

Corners stepped to the floor. "It's okay McNally," he placated. "He's too stupid to know any better. And I make allowances for stupidity."

His glowering eyes did not support his easy tone as he moved across the saloon, with his deputies side-stepping to have clear shots around him at Edge.

"Your allowance is an hour, drifter," the big man continued as he approached the halfbreed. "Only one man could have killed George Bradbury. That's you. Murder in the first degree I'd say."

Edge's gleaming teeth and glinting eyes seemed to generate a physical force that brought Corners to a halt six feet away from him. The Winchester was still held low pointing at the floor. The Colt aimed at Corners' flat, hard-looking belly.

"You're still in town after an hour, I'll arrest you," the big man challenged.

Beads of sweat coursed down the freshly-shaved faces of both men. Neither raised a hand to brush away the moisture. The droplets splashed from their jaws to their shirt fronts.

"You're gonna just let him ride out?" Dorrie gasped. "After what he done?"

The blood had dried in a sheet on her lower face. As she twisted her features into a look of hate a thousand tiny cracks appeared in the slick red covering.

"Keep quiet, Dorrie," Corners said with soft-voiced anger that was no longer directed entirely at Edge. "I've no doubt you had a hand in starting the trouble here."

"Wouldn't say that," Edge drawled.

"She did too!" Billy yelled.

"Not a hand," Edge told Corners. "It's that mouth of hers."

The half-breed released the Winchester and the clatter it made against the floor caused an instant of startlement within everyone in the saloon. Dorrie was frozen in mid-stride as she took her first step away from the bar. In that moment, Edge was the only man to move. He went forward, clear of Bradbury's body. Corners leaned back in alarm, mouth springing open to yell an order. The cold grin was still carved on Edge's face.

"Your offer sounds a good one sheriff," the half-breed said, and holstered his Colt.

The action of apparent surrender extended the moment of surprise caused by the unexpected noise. Then Edge began to raise his hands and instead of a command, it was a hiss of amazement that issued from Corner's mouth. The deputies' trigger fingers were white with tension as they crooked around the metal.

"Mr. Edge!" Billy muttered in disgust.

The half-breed sprang to the side, his left arm forming into a wide hook and his right hand flashing to the back of his neck. His splayed feet thudded to the floor behind Dorrie as she started forward again. His left arm hooked around her body just beneath her thrusting breasts. His right hand rested across her shoulder, clenched into a fist around the handle of the razor. The blade, gleaming brighter than the lawmen's badges in the lamplight, was laid against the woman's throat.

"Don't!" Corners implored with a roar.

"Like I say" Edge responded evenly as the deputies leaned forward, pushing out their guns but not daring to tighten their curled fingers. "Sounds a good offer. But I'm overbidding, feller. Putting up the dame's life for what it's worth. You get to keep your hour. I'll ride out now."

"You didn't trust him!" Billy yelled, filled with joy again.

"Not on your life, Billy," Edge replied. "which won't be a long one if you stick around in Hate."

"Uncle Luke?" Dorrie pleaded breathlessly as Edge's tight grip constricted her lungs.

"What's the deal?" Corners snarled from the depths of his angry frustration.

"The muscle toss their guns out of the door," Edge instructed.

"Do it!" Corners barked, not taking his dark eyes off the lean face of the half-breed, still sweat-

47

run and speckled with the spots of blood which had sprayed from Dorrie's wound.

The tacit excitement generated by the group of men at the far end of the bar seemed to vibrate in the hot air which reeked of exploded powder from the shotgun blast. The deputies hesitated only a moment before reluctantly turning to toss their guns out into the street.

"Now what?" Corners demanded.

Dorrie began to tremble against Edge. A pulse started to work frantically in her throat and then she struggled to hold her breath as the honed sharpness of the razor dug into her flesh.

"Billy?" Edge said.

"Yes, sir, Mr. Edge," the simple-minded man replied at once his moon face breaking out into a smile. He had been sunk into a slough of depression since Edge had warned him of the repercussions of his participation.

"Pick up the money I left on the bar" Edge told him. "That's your stake."

"Couldn't do that, Mr. Edge," Billy replied ruefully, shaking his head.

Edge could not see the expression or the negative action. But he picked up the tone and an icy anger showed in his hooded eyes. "Why the hell not?" he demanded acidly.

"Ain't done nothin' to earn no money Mr. Edge."

"Advance payment," Edge told him. "To earn it, you come out from behind the bar, pick up my rifle and take it outside."

"I can sure do that" Billy announced, gleeful once more. He began to shovel the loose change into his pocket.

"Then you hook the rifle on to the saddle of one

48

of the deputies' horses, Billy," Edge went on. "Don't matter which one. Mr. Corners wouldn't let any of his help ride a broken down nag, I guess."

"After murder, horse-stealing's nothing," Corners muttered grimly as Billy climbed over the bar and scooped up the fallen Winchester.

Edge formed his lips into a tight line to hide his teeth, then pursed them and spat. The globule of moisture hit the floor between the big man's highly polished boots. "I'm a real mean bastard," he rasped, and cracked the smile again. "Guess I got to hang now."

"Billy, don't do it!" the elder McNally croaked as his son moved fearfully between the docile mare and tense deputies to reach the doorway.

Neither Billy nor anyone else paid attention to the old man's plaintive plea.

"You won't hang, drifter," Corners snarled. "You'll die a lot slower than that when I catch up with you."

The white mare emptied her bowels. She lifted her tail and the dung exploded from her. Steam rose from the heaped mess in the doorway and emanated its nauseatingly sweet stench into the saloon.

"Not exactly from the horse's mouth, feller," Edge replied, taking a step forward and forcing Dorrie to move ahead of him. "But she sure enough said it for me."

He steered the terrified woman on a curving course, swinging wide of Corners. The big man turned to watch Edge and his captive every inch of the way. The deputies barring passage to the door held their positions for a few moments, then stepped aside. All four flicked their expectant gazes from Corners to Edge and back again.

"How far are you taking her?" the big man demanded.

"All ready, Mr. Edge!" Billy called from outside. "The black gelding."

"Obliged," Edge replied. "Now beat it, feller."

He had kept his back to the bystanders on the slow, shuffling route to the doorway. But he knew there was nothing to fear from that direction: aware that only the danger of reprisals held the men from doing more than willing him to escape Corners' vengeance.

"How far are you taking her?" the big man repeated, snarling, almost trembling with rage.

Edge halted in the doorway and spread a thoughtful frown across his lean features. "Used to be a fine-looking woman," he said reflectively. "Might have been different then. Now, I don't reckon I'd like to go all the way with her."

"Give me an answer, man!" Corners ranted his anger putting a high pitch on his voice.

The half-breed nodded. "Don't want no excess baggage," he said, curling a leg around her ankles and releasing his arm from around her. Then he withdrew the razor from her throat and shoved hard against her shoulder.

With a shriek of alarm Dorrie tripped over Edge's leg and crashed down across the threshold: plunging her head into the sticky heap of fresh horse droppings.

Corners bellowed like a wild animal and the deputies lunged and crashed between the tables and chairs to retrieve their guns. Edge whirled and reached the black gelding in two strides. As he swung up into the saddle he saw a large crowd of people gathered in front of the courthouse, silent and wan-faced in the silvered moonlight. He plunged the razor back into the neck pouch and reached for the Winchester jutting from the boot.

"No sweat, mister!" a man called tonelessly from the rear of the crowd. "About time somebody dropped that bitch in it."

Edge heeled the gelding into a full-stretch gallop. He headed west because that was the way the horse was facing and was clattering across the trestle bridge as the four deputies lunged out of the saloon. Their Colts crackled, but the bullets decayed into the dust long before reaching the out-of-range target of the halfbreed.

"Mr. Edge!" a voice called from out of the moon shade of-range target of the half-breed.

Edge hauled on the reins to bring the gelding to a skidding stop as the panting Billy stepped out on to the trail ahead of him.

"Two up'll slow me," the half-breed told the man harshly.

"Ain't all that much rush, Mr. Edge," Billy said with a grin, forcing out the words between gasps for breath. "I ain't all that bright. But I ain't all that stupid either. I fixed it so you'd have more time."

Billy drew a knife from the back of his belt and showed it to Edge. The half-breed eyed the glinting blade, then snapped his head around to look back across the bridge to the front of The Last Drop Hotel. He was in time to see three of the deputies leap towards their horses. Then, as they tried to lever themselves up, the stirrups plunged under their weight, dragging the saddles from the backs of the horses.

"Guess that ought to slow 'em up some, Mr.

Edge," Billy yelled as the deputies collapsed hard into the dust of the street.

Edge cracked lips in a humorless grin as he reached out a hand to haul the man up on to the horse behind him. "Guess you could say that's a clear-cut cinch, Billy," he replied.

CHAPTER FOUR

EDGE and his simple-minded passenger were long gone by the time the three deputies had commandered new saddles and the fourth lawman had replaced his stolen horse. While the near-insanely enraged Corners used his mare to carry the hysterical Dorrie to the lumber mill, the quartet galloped over the bridge and out on to the trail. Corners bellowed a warning to them—not to come back into town unless they had the drifter with them. Then he carried the sobbing woman up the long stairway to the living quarters on the top floor of the mill.

The grim-faced deputies had clear sign to follow on the trail through the scattered tree stumps for the gelding with two men up left deep impressions in the dust of the long summer. But amid the towering pines on the rising ground, deep shadow cloaked the trail. The deputies were a half mile into the trees, nearing the crest of the rise, when they realized their quarry had veered to the side. The tracks left by their own horses obliterated those which had been imprinted by the gelding and it was a tediously slow chore to find the point at which Edge had spurred away from the trail. And even when they found the traces they were looking for, the near dense blackness within the forest made further tracking impossible before morning.

Fearful of catching the backlash of Corners' residual anger, the four men smoked several cigarettes in tense silence: stretching out the wasted time to a duration that they hoped would appear reasonable to the big man. Then they started back along the trail to town: breaking into a gallop when they saw the unmistakable silhouette of Corners outlined against a lighted window on the top of the lumber mill.

"He looks mad, even from here," one of the men called above the beat of hooves.

"The hell with it," a red-headed man responded. "It's worth a balling out."

"How's that?" the deputy with the cleft chin wanted to know.

"Seeing that stuck-up bitch of a niece covered in horseshit."

The squint-eyed man who had commented on Corners' appearance at the window spat into the slipstream. "That weren't nothin' to what's gonna be flying around 'til the boss sees the drifter dead," he predicted.

"Which ain't gonna be one easy thing to see," the fourth galloping rider muttered to himself, with a grimace that emphasized the livid knife scar under his left eye.

Edge was not thinking of either life or death as Billy McNally slid to the ground and pointed toward the cabin crouched at one side of a small clearing in the pine trees.

"Ain't nobody but me knows about this place, Mr. Edge," the man announced proudly, a broad beam on his moon face.

The half-breed was thinking about food and sleep and before he slid from the saddle he had decided that the simpleton's hideaway offered good prospect of fulfilling the latter need.

"You sure of that, feller?" he asked.

He raked his eyes around the clearing and settled his hooded gaze upon Billy. The man's smile faded fast and he hung his head and shuffled his feet.

"Well, Mr. Edge . . . I guess it's just 'cause I figure it for my special place than I tell myself no one else knows about it." He looked up suddenly and started to speak fast, his dark, normally placid eyes shining. "But I ain't never seen no one else up here 'cepting my Pa, Mr. Edge. When he comes lookin' for me after I've been missin' for a couple of days."

Edge looked long at Billy, then cracked the kind of smile that came as close as he was able to display amusement. "No sweat, feller," he placated gently hanging the gelding's reins forward across the animal's head. He slid the Winchester from the boot and started toward the cabin. "It's just got to be safer than a room at The Long Drop, I guess."

There was no lock on the door and just the single window at the front. It had been built a long time ago and showed many signs of inexpert repair. The roof and walls had been patched in several places by nailing odd lengths of timber over the holes.

"See how I fixed it up to keep it warm and dry, Mr. Edge?" Billy said excitedly, proudly.

"You did a good job," Edge allowed absently as he pushed open the door. He struck a match on the jamb and held it aloft. There was just the one room furnished with a table, chair and bunk. The furniture looked as ill-used as the cabin. On the bunk was an ancient mattress that seemed to have lost most of its feather guts before several rents were roughly stitched together. There was a pot-bellied stove against one wall.

As Edge crossed the threshold, Billy darted around him and crouched down beside the bunk. He dragged a cardboard carton out from underneath and Edge saw the shine of several cans before the match went out.

"Supplies," Billy announced. "You're welcome to use 'em, Mr. Edge. Ain't got no labels on 'em, so don't know what's in 'em."

"It'll make meal-times fun," Edge replied not bothering with another match.

The first one had shown that the door and window at the front of the cabin were indeed, the only means of entry and exit. And when the effect of the match flare had faded and his eyes became accustomed to the gloom, enough moonlight penetrated the dirt-grimed window to show him the layout of the single room.

"All right I leave now, Mr. Edge?" Billy asked. "Long way to go."

"Where?" Edge wanted to know.

"Trasker. Thirty miles west of Corners."

The simple-minded man had no horse or gun. And no more than a dollar and a half in loose change. All he had going for him was the weather and determination.

"Luck to you," Edge told him, turning to go out through the door.

Billy came out of the cabin as the half-breed was starting to unsaddle the gelding. "I'm gonna make it this time, Mr. Edge," he said.

"You gotta believe it," Edge replied as he unbuckled the cinch.

"Tried it better than ten times already. Best I did before Pa caught up with me was fifteen miles. But this time I'm gonna make it."

He sounded confident but his unintelligent face betrayed a kind of pathetic need for something. Edge slid the saddle from the back of the gelding and carried it into the cabin. When he re-emerged, Billy was still standing on the same spot.

"Reckon I'll be movin' on now, Mr. Edge," he said.

Edge nodded catching hold of the reins of the horse.

"Wished I had a gun," Billy said. "Ain't easy to catch food on the run with just a knife."

"Keep practising," Edge told him, and led the gelding around to the rear of the cabin.

There was a water barrel there under a down pipe from the roof gutter. It was filled with old rain that looked dirty. But the horse drank gratefully after Edge had ground hobbled him. When the half-breed returned to the front of the cabin, Billy McNally was standing in the middle of the clearing.

"I figured we was friends, Mr. Edge," he called his tone heavy with sadness. "You got a rifle and a handgun both."

"It's that kind of unequal world, Billy," Edge told him.

"Pa always says a friend in need is a friend indeed," the simpleton challenged.

Edge sighed. "Your Pa ain't so bright either," he responded. "A friend in need is the kind to stay away from."

Even across the distance that separated them, Edge could see the anger twisting Billy's features.

57

I'm sorry I ever helped you, Mr. Edge," he snarled, and whirled around. His stride was purposeful.

"Billy!" Edge called.

The man halted and turned happy relief flooding his features. "Yeah, Mr. Edge?"

"One favor deserves another."

"That sure is right, Mr. Edge."

He started forward, on the point of breaking into a run. But Edge halted him abruptly by raising a hand, palm outwards.

"You said Trasker's west of here?"

Billy nodded, Edge's stance, expression and tone of voice causing his delight to abate rapidly. Edge folded his raised hand into a fist then jutted out his index finger and swung his arm to point in the opposite direction to the one Billy had been headed for.

"West is that way" the halfbreed said.

Billy was bewildered for a moment, then he turned again, and started off in the direction Edge was indicating. "Real sorry what I done for you!" the simpleton shouted back. "You ain't no better than Corners and his men."

"I'm better," Edge muttered, low so that only he could hear the words. "I'm still living."

Then he went into the cabin and closed the door. He moved to the window and watched the tall, frail-looking Billy until the simpleton had gone from sight into the trees, then he moved along each wall of the cabin, testing the strength of the timber with the butt of his Colt. There was an area of damp rottenness at the rear, but it was not extensive enough for anything better than a jack-rabbit to burrow through. In the rear slope of the low pitch roof there was a patched hole large enough

58

© Lorillard 1975

If you have a taste for quality, you'll like the taste of Kent.

King Size or Deluxe 100's.

KENT
WITH
THE FAMOUS MICRONITE FILTER

KING SIZE

KING SIZE
KENT

Kings: 16 mg. "tar," 1.0 mg. nicotine; 100's: 18 mg. "tar," 1.2 mg. nicotine av. per cigarette, FTC Report Oct.'74.

Newport

Alive with pleasure!

Newport
20
CLASS A
CIGARETTES

Newport®

MENTHOL KINGS

for a man to gain entry or exit. The table was stronger than the chair and gave Edge sufficient height to reach the roof with ease. It needed only slight pressure to force up the timber repair, the nails creaking free. He allowed the boarding to slide down the slope into the guttering. Then he climbed down to the dirt floor, leaving the table beneath the hole, and dragged the bunk across to the window.

The humidity seemed to get higher as the night grew older and he sweated a lot. More salty moisture coursed his flesh as he hammered open two of the cans from the carton, using the butt of the Colt. Then the sweat dried as he sat on the side of the bunk and ate a meal of cold beans and salted beef, scooping the food from the jagged cans with his fingers. He felt no sense of loss or regret about the spartanly comfortable room at The Last Drop or the restaurant on the other side of the doorway in the saloon. A combination of circumstances outside his control and his reactions to them had removed such relative luxuries out of reach. He accepted such events as the facts of his kind of life.

The meal over, he drew the Winchester from the saddle boot and leaned it against the side of the bunk. Then he stretched out on the slack mattress, fully-dressed to the extent of not removing his gunbelt. He pushed his hat forward over his face to hide the pale moonlight from his eyes. Then he went to sleep: taking the kind of rest that was just as much a heritage of the violent years as everything about the man when awake. Sleep came fast, to make the most of however little time he would be allowed to rest. And it was shallow, his brain and body drawing refreshment without being fully relaxed. So that his mind was constantly alert to pick up signs of threatened danger and his physical responses were poised to take avoiding action.

Thus it was that he heard the approach of the rider and snapped open his eyes. For only a part of a second he stared into the pitch dark of the under side of his hat: his waking mind sliding smoothly into action from the trigger of the danger warning. He strained his ears to pin-point the direction from which the man was coming, then began to rise: tipping the hat on to his head and reaching for the Winchester.

He had so positioned the bunk that as he sat up, he could see the entire clearing from the window. It had been the snap of a dried twig under a hoof that had penetrated into his state of sleeping awareness. Now he heard the pine needle-muffled progress of the horse for several seconds before animal and rider came into view. The high moon shone a gentle, silvered light across the clearing and showed the man as a black silhouette against the less solid darkness of the pine. The barrel of the rifle he was holding gleamed with a dull sheen.

Edge watched from the window as the man dismounted and hitched his horse to a tree branch before stalking toward the cabin. Then the half-breed swung his feet to the dirt floor, rose and reached the table in two strides. He climbed up, reached through the hole in the roof and hauled himself out. He was as silent as a shadow and his movements were just as soundless as he inched up the slope of the roof and peered over the peak. The intruder was half-way across the clearing and had halted, some thirty feet from the front of the cabin.

The eyes of the half-breed flicked to left and right, checking that the intruder was alone.

"Hey!" the man called softly, nervously. "Mr. Edge? You in there, Mr. Edge?"

The half-breed did not reply and, in the pause, the surrounding forest seemed to throb with the tension of silenced nature.

"I don't mean you no harm, Mr. Edge!" the man went on, his voice louder. His fear was more apparent.

The heavy, expectant silence clamped down again and the man seemed rooted to the spot. Edge sensed he was torn between turning and fleeing on the run or striding towards the cabin. But when he moved it was to shuffle forward: in the awkward manner of a tall man forcing him self to take short steps. His rifle was canted across the front of his body, pointed to the sky.

"I was sent by the Citizens Committee, Mr. Edge," he called, on the verge of stuttering as fear tightened a grip on his throat. "Name's Maclean, I got picked. Didn't want to come out here. You in there, Mr. Edge?"

Silence for a reply as he came within twenty feet of the cabin.

"Honest, Mr. Edge. You ain't gotta worry about me."

"What are you worried about, feller?" Edge drawled.

The man was rooted to the spot now, held by a bolt of terror in an awkward posture of mid-stride. Unevenly balanced as if a mere breath of air would topple him. He tilted his head to look up at the roof and the moonlight bounced off a thousand beads of sweat standing out against his face. His wide eyes and gaping mouth looked like depthless pits against the wet, pale surround of the skin. Edge recognized him as a member of the second group of men who had entered the saloon.

His mouth closed and opened several times before he could force out the taut words. "Hell, you near scared me to death!"

"Ain't a reliable method," Edge replied, pulling the Winchester up from his side and drawing a bead on the man. "Never replace this one."

The man began to quake. "Please, Mr. Edge!" he begged. "I didn't want to come. We drew lots. I'm just a dentist for Christ sake."

"We're in the same business, in a manner of speaking," Edge said.

Maclean gulped. "What?"

Edge didn't take his hooded eyes off the man below him. He pursed his lips, then sucked them in and spat. It was a direct hit into the gutter at the front of the cabin. "You don't drop that rifle I might just drill you, feller. Filling'll be the lead kind."

Maclean stared at his rifle for a stretched second, then hurled it away from him as though it were hot. "Only brought it in case I was spotted leaving town and they trailed me," he explained hurriedly.

"Careful men lead longer lives," Edge told him, maintaining the aim of the Winchester. It was pleasant up on the roof, a little cooler than inside the cabin. "But there are exceptions to every rule. How'd you know I was here, feller?"

"Cyrus McNally's on the Citizens Committee, Mr. Edge. Lots of folks saw you ride off with Billy up behind you. Cyrus told us Billy often come to

62

this old place when he'd done somethin' wrong. We figured it was worth a try."

"Try for what?"

Maclean still seemed incapable of moving his feet. But he was able to raise an arm and wipe away most of the sweat on his face with a shirt sleeve. "Find you and warn you Luke Corners ain't the kind of man to forget a grudge, Mr. Edge."

Edge nodded. "Obliged. Be obliged again if you'd beat it and let me get back to sleep."

"Weren't all I come for, Mr. Edge," the dentist hurried on.

"Talk's almost as cheap as life," the half-breed invited. "But lost sleep could be too high a price to pay unless I got something I don't already have."

Maclean swallowed hard. "Corners has posted a reward for you, Mr. Edge. Five thousand dollars. And not just to his deputies. Woke up the whole town to make the announcement. And he told us he's sent one of his boys into Trasker. To hire some gunslingers. He figures to have you hunted down no matter where you go."

Edge thought about this for a moment and the forest came alive with low volume noise again as the animals and insects adapted to the voices of the men and recommenced their nocturnal business.

"Still ain't all," Edge said at length. "Folks of Hate don't owe me anything. Even a warning."

Maclean pumped his head in agreement. "That's right, Mr. Edge. But it sure did the folks some good to see the way you stood up to Corners and give him the run around, the bastard."

"Weren't for anybody's benefit but mine," Edge told him.

"That don't matter," Maclean said quickly as he

suspected Edge was about to continue. "It got folks to thinkin'. We lived so long with that bastard runnin' us we got to believe there weren't no other way. But you showed us different, Mr. Edge."

Edge sighed. "You gonna get to the point, or are you just here to needle me, feller?"

"We can raise a thousand dollars," Maclean blurted out.

"Don't reckon that'll be enough to buy him off," the half-breed replied wryly.

"For you to run Corners and his boys outta town," Maclean went on as if there had been no interruption. "Be in your interest, too. Apart from the money. Especially if you kill the bastard. Then he won't be around to hire no guns to go lookin' for you, Mr. Edge."

Edge did not take time to consider the offer and he spoke with the easy confidence of a man whose hip pocket bulged with the best part of five thousand dollars. "Go back to Hate and raise the money, feller."

Delight spread across the upturned face. "Sure thing, Mr. Edge." He started to turn.

"Then!" Edge called, louder.

The dentist swung his attention back to the half-breed. "Yeah?" Excitedly.

"Roll each bill up tight," Edge replied. "And stick them up the collective ass of the Citizens Committee."

Maclean's moment of happiness was frozen on his sweat-run features for long seconds. Then the abysmal depths of his disappointment became evident.

"Sorry you been troubled," he said dejectedly.

"Likewise," Edge told him coldly.

"Can I take my rifle?"

"Sure. You might be able to use it to shove those bills where I told you. Won't be no guts to——"

"I got the message of what you think of us," Maclean cut in. Then he stopped, picked up the rifle, turned and strode back to where his horse was hitched.

The rifle shot cracked obscenely across the low murmur of forest sound. There was no echo and the split-second of silence that followed the explosion was absolute. Then Maclean punctured it with a ghastly scream. He had one foot in the stirrup and was hoisting himself up on to the horse. The bullet took him in the jaw on a rising trajectory, burrowing through the flesh, amashing into his lower teeth and then tunneling upwards to burst open the roof of his mouth and kick into his brain. It was a very shrill, very short scream. Then he was silent in death as the impact of the bullet sailed his twitching body through the air and thudded it to the ground.

The half-breed saw nothing of this. He heard the gunshot, saw the brief flare of a muzzle flash, then angled his body to the side and rolled down the slope of the roof. Macleans scream split the humid air as Edge smacked into the gutter. He powered himself down to land on his feet just as the dead man thudded to the ground.

The shot had come from the trees on the left on the clearing. Edge went towards the right, running around the nervously snorting horse and angling away from the cabin to keep its bulk between himself and the rifleman until he reached the cover of the trees. The grass of the open space muffled his footfalls at first, then he was on the deep carpet of

65

pine needles. Once in the protection of the tall up-
rights of the trunks, he changed direction. He
walked now, taking long strides, doubling back
across the rear of the cabin. The shot and the
scream which followed it had a more traumatic effect on the creatures of the forest than had the
voices of the men. It took a full minute for the low
murmuring to begin again and by that time the
half-breed was in the trees at the side of the clearing, thirty feet back from where he had seen the
flash of the exploded shell. He was as motionless as
the trees all around him, ears straining for the
slightest sound which struck an alien note.

When it came, it was a gentle thud—on the far
side of the clearing. The narrowed eyes glinted in
recognition and the thin lips curled in the familiar
humorless grin. Maclean's killer was a crack shot
with a rifle but lacked the ability for original
thought. He had tossed a small rock in an attempt
to mislead the half-breed.

Edge moved forward, flitting like a silent shadow. He remained erect and zig-zagged from tree to
tree, merging into the cover of each knarled trunk
as he reached it. At each brief halt, he looked out
into the clearing, to where Maclean's horse stood
like a statue beside the slumped body of the dentist.
Moonlight made a bright pool of the animal's eye
and emphasized the taut black points of the pricked
ears. The horse's fearful attention was riveted upon
the spot among the trees where Edge felt certain the
rifle man was waiting.

The half-breed took three more silent strides,
then froze as a rustling noise reached him. The
horse snorted and the gelding behind the cabin responded in like manner. Edge saw the small, dark

rock sail across the clearing: heard the more muffled sound as it missed the pines and impacted with the time-rotted needles. He was within ten feet of the man now. He stepped to the side and saw him.

A bulky man, hunched into a crouch, looking towards the cabin but hidden from it. Exposed at the rear and sides. Edge blinked sweat beads from his eyelashes and raised the Winchester stock to his shoulder.

"Pull that trigger and you'll sprout wings—about here!"

The voice was soft, but clear, speaking from close behind Edge. A gun muzzle thudded into the center of the half-breed's back as the man spoke the final word. The crouching man swung his head around and Edge recognized the features formed into an evil grin—the deputy with the knife scar beneath his right eye. It took just an instant of thought to decide Edge's reaction to the voice and gun. Maclean had been killed instead of him. To flush him out into the open and get the drop on him. Words and the solid threat of the gun. Corners wanted him alive. In the next instant a man died. He ended his life with a grin and a broken heart. Edge squeezed the trigger and the bullet smashed into the deputy's chest just below his tin star. It rifled through the rapidly beating heart, stopping it instantly. Then it burst clear at the back, chased out by a gush of crimson.

Again the half-breed had no time to see the effect of a rifle shot. Corners' wish would not have precedence over a man's ardent desire to survive. The man behind him was confident his order would be obeyed and Edge had to grasp the slim advantage of shattering surprise to implement his

67

own instinct for self-preservation. In the sliver of time it took the man's mind to adjust to the totally unexpected, Edge acted. He folded forward from the waist and launched a vicious back heel. The man fired his rifle and Edge felt the bullet ripple the hairs on the nape of his neck before it bored a hole in his hat brim.

The heel of his boot sank into the sparse flesh beneath the man's kneecap and he screamed. Edge forced himself to fall sideways, turning his body as he went down. He thudded to the ground in a splayed-legged sitting position, the ready-cocked Winchester aimed. The deputy with the cleft chin was sunk on to his hurt knee, his face contorted by pain and terror as his hands scrabbled at the level action of his rifle.

"No chance, feller," Edge warned softly.

The deputy forced down the lever. Edge squeezed the trigger. The bullet smashed into the crooked knee of the good leg. It splintered the bone to the accompaniment of a wailing scream and burrowed through the flesh encasing the femur. The man fell backwards, flinging his rifle high into the air and reaching both hands to his new injury. He continued to vent his agony as Edge climbed casually to his feet and stepped across to tower above the shaking body. The piercing sound did not stop until the muzzle of the half-breed's Winchester was lowered against the pulsing throat. The whites of the man's near popping eyes seemed to gleam with the light of the agony coursing through him.

"Please?" he pleaded, his voice a harsh croak. "It was Christian's idea." Saliva bubbled out of the corner of his mouth and ran down his chin.

"What's religion got to do with it?" Edge muttered sardonically, steadying the rifle as the man's Adam's apple bobbed.

"My buddy!" the deputy whined through clenched teeth. "Frederick H. Christian. He figured we could trail the dentist and get led to you. I just come along to——"

"Fit me with a pair of wings," Edge cut in. "But turns out Fred's an angel all of a sudden."

"What d'you want with me, mister?" the agony-wracked deputy implored. "Gee——

"Report," Edge barked.

"What?"

"Fill me in," the half-breed explained the same harsh tones. "How'd he know Mclean was headed out to find me?"

"He had an in with the Citizens Committee," the man replied quickly, anxious to comply in the hope that the half-breed towering above him would show compassion.

"Who?"

"Honest, I don't know, mister." The possibility that he would survive transcended his pain and the deputy's voice was stronger. More ingratiating. "If I knew, no reason why I shouldn't tell you?"

"Guess that's right," Edge agreed. "So we got nothing else to talk about."

Terror seemed to rise from the deputy in visible waves, like heat shimmer in a desert. "Don't shoot me, mister?" he pleaded.

"Okay," Edge said easily.

Relief expanded a wet stain from the crotch of the deputy's pants. Edge tilted the Winchester away from the pulsing throat. Then he powered down into a stoop, his left hand streaking to the back of his neck. It came away even faster, with a metallic flash from the moonlight on the blade. The action was so swift the man on the ground did not have time to reflect his fear on his face. The point of the razor plunged into the flesh beneath one of his ears and went deep. Edge drew the blade in a vicious arc and did not pull it clear until it nicked the lobe of the other ear. The deputy died showing an expression caught between terror and joy. Blood gushed from the gaping wound as if from an undammed red river. But the flow had stopped by the time the half-breed had wiped the razor clean on the corpse's shirt.

"Condemned man deserves a last request," he murmured, then went back into the cabin to resume his interrupted sleep.

CHAPTER FIVE

IN even the hottest of summers there is a brief period during the false dawn of each new day when the air is cool. It is as if nature seeks to reassure all living things on earth that the unremitting sun which is shortly to rise will eventually exhaust its heat for the year and they can exist in comfort again. During such a period, if a man is awake to reflect, he is inclined to accept the interlude at face value and not consider the potential harshness of the winter which can be far more cruel than any summer.

Edge awoke at the beginning of the false dawn, when the stars went out as the sky changed from black to grey in advance of the sun's leading arc. Surrounded by the richness of natural things—the white crest of the distant mountain ridges; the glimmer of dark blue from the far off lake; the deep green of the towering pines; the singing of birds; and the luxury of the fresh, clear, cool air—he thought about the bullet hole in the brim of his hat.

He battered open a tin from the carton of supplies and tossed it into the heap of dead ashes in the stove when the stink of rottenness rose from the mouldy beans inside. He needed a new hat and decided he could also do with a decent meal. As he carried the saddle from the cabin, he saw that Macleans's horse had wandered into the center of the clearing and was grazing with two other geldings:

still saddled from when the deputies had left them to go stalking five thousand dollars. The dentist still lay where he had fallen, of course, his putrefying flesh giving off an evil odor into the freshness of the air. The corpses of the deputies were presumably still among the trees where they had died.

Edge carried the saddle around to the rear of the cabin and dunked his head into the rain water barrel before preparing the horse for riding. The sun hauled its advance curve above the tree tops in the east as he rode out into the clearing and the moisture dried from his face. Then the sweat of exertion replaced it as he coaxed the dead men's horses to him and loaded the evil-smelling corpses across the saddles. The bodies hung limply, arms and legs dangling: the humidity which had hastened decomposition had slowed down the stiffening process of rigor.

It was not, of course, the desire to buy a new hat and the need for a good meal which turned Edge eastwards, cracking his eyes against the glare of the newly-risen sun. The town called Hate was doubtless the nearest community but there had to be other places on the Continental Divide where he could get what he wanted. But they did not have Luke Corners living in them—the man who was offering a five grand reward for the half-breed.

Being a wanted fugitive with a price on his head was not a new experience for Edge. It was a reward, posted in Kansas, for his capture to stand trial for the killing of a man named Elliot Thombs which had caused him to forsake his given name and to flee the land which was his birthright.* But

* See—Edge: The Loner.

72

that had been a long time ago and the hundred dollars offered was not enough to keep the bounty hunters interested. Five thousand was a different proposition entirely. With that kind of money riding on his head, a man had to be destined for an early grave.

It was seven o'clock when Edge rode at an easy pace out of the trees, leading the three horses with their putrid burdens. The sun was well clear of the foothills now, blazing down fiercely upon the town, the river and the vast area of tree-stripped ground littered with the naked stumps of felled pines. The harsh heat easily penetrated the dark pall of wood-smoke which was suspended above the town, fed by the cooking fires which burned beneath every chimney.

As the half-breed and his charges moved out across the open country it was as if every man in Hate emerged to meet him. They came out of the houses at the far end of the single street to form an enlarging group which moved at a shuffling, somehow dejected, pace toward the bridge. Because he was better than a half mile away, Edge could not hear the sound of their progress, at first muffled by the dust they dragged up from the street, then clattering as their boots thudded against the boards of the bridge.

The group halted at the big gates in the fence surrounding the lumber mill just as Edge reached a marker sign he had not noticed on his rapid retreat from the town last night. It was a very elaborate sign, neatly painted with expertly-shaped lettering and a symbolic picture.

YOU ARE NOW ENTERING
THE FORMER TOWN OF THEA
RENAMED CORNERS
IN HONOR OF ITS PREMIER CITIZEN
AND GEOGRAPHICAL SITUATION

Beneath the lettering was a pictorial representation of the valley intersection with the river running across it. The high angles of the valleys were exaggerated to emphasize why Luke Corners was gracious enough to share his honor with topography. The message came across clearly to the tall half-breed—as did the anagram of Thea which produced the equally appropriate town name fading on the marker at the side of the east trail.

Edge paused only a moment to look at the sign, then heeled his horse forward again. The almost eerie impression that the men of the town had been coming out to meet him was totally destroyed as he shaded his hooded eyes with a brown-skinned hand and saw that the group was turned to face the mill gates. As he drew closer, a man in the group spotted him and there was a ripple of movement as every pair of eyes was turned toward the half-breed. A murmur of conversation trembled in the hot air: then was silenced by a shout. All attention was returned to the gates and Edge's slitted eyes swung to peer through the wire mesh fence at the mill.

The massive figure of Luke Corners towered above the flanking forms of his two remaining deputies as the trio strode between the mill and the gates. The old men carried a burlap sack. Winchesters were canted in the crooked arms of the men on either side of him. The deputies swung open the gates and Corners stood like a craggy outcrop of rock in the center of the entrance just as Edge halted his own and the pack animals at the side of the group of men. For the last two hundred yards, the half-breed had been riding with his rifle drawn, canted across the front of his body in a one-handed grip.

The big man on the horse and the big man on the ground clashed eyes across the heads of the anxious faced men between them. Controlled anger twisted the features of Corners. Edge appeared coldly at ease.

"You ain't welcome in this town, drifter!" The words were spat out, as though they had an evil taste.

The deputies waited by the gates, poised to fling themselves into the cover they offered. The waiting men hung their heads, bodies rigid with tension.

"Heard you were real anxious to have me back, sheriff," Edge replied evenly. "Five grand anxious."

"Talking out the back of your head," Corners retorted.

A few of the men in the group looked at the half-breed now. Their faces were blank, suggesting they had no intention of contradicting Corners or explaining the change of attitude.

"Hole's in the back of my hat, not my head," Edge said. "Should have convinced me your deputy wasn't a straight shooter."

"You killed those men?" Corners asked. Completely in control of himself. The effort didn't even show and his voice was pitched evenly, holding a note of indifference.

Edge did not understand the new mood of the

big man, but he sensed it was no part of a trick. He slid the Winchester back in the boot and saw the tension leave the expressions of the deputies as they moved to take up positions on either side of Corners. He hauled on the reins of each trailing horse in turn, and displayed the face of each dead man by yanking his head up with a fistful of hair.

"Him . . . and him," he admitted as, first the man with a bullet through his heart and then the one with a slit throat, was exhibited. "Self-defense, sheriff. After one of 'em had a brush with Maclean." He held up the head of the dead dentist, the mouth gaping to show the stumps of the shattered lower teeth imbedded in the crust of congealed blood. The ugly blackness of the dried blood emphasized the ghastly paleness of the dead man's complexion.

"Don't tell me about it," Corners rasped. "I'm not the top law in town today." He delved a meaty hand into the sack and withdrew a cardboard tag. "Number thirty-five!" he yelled.

A man at the rear of the group pushed to the front and went through the gateway. He didn't smile, but there was something about his walk that suggested a mild degree of happiness.

"Eighteen!" Corners called as he drew out another tag.

A second man responded by going through into the lumber mill. Edge watched in cool detachment as the process of random selection continued. In the mounting heat of morning, the mill wheel churned, flies droned as they swarmed about the bloodied wounds of the dead, Corners' voice spat out numbers and men shuffled through the dust. Then:

"That's it," the big, silver-haired man proclaimed. "Just need twenty-five hands today."

Ten were left on the wrong side of the gates. One of these—fifty, stooped-shouldered and with a haggard face upon which the skin hung in loose folds—scuttled forward.

"Mr. Corners!" he whined. "I ain't done no work in ten days. I got a wife and kids to—"

Corners nodded curtly to one of the deputies as he spun around. The deputy stepped forward, thrusting the Winchester out in front of him. The bent old man saw the coming attack in time to halt, but he had no chance of turning away from it. The rifle muzzle thudded into the base of his stomach and he screamed, high and thin. He folded forward and the deputy spun the rifle. The top of the stock crashed into the head of the winded man, who pitched into the dust, silent and pouring blood from a split in his bald dome. None of the other rejected men moved, held still by the raking swing of the second deputy's Winchester.

"Haul him out of here and learn!" the lawman who had done the damage snarled, backing away and levelling his rifle. "You all know the rules. Break 'em and you get broke."

Every man in the group wore a holstered gun, but the deputies turned their backs with complete confidence and began to hustle the chosen workers towards the mill with the parked wagons aligned outside. Two of the rejected men stooped to lift the injured one between them.

"Bastards!" a tough-looking young man who was naked to the waist muttered, and spat into the dust.

"That's really scaring the hell out of 'em," Edge

taunted as he heeled the gelding forward, jerking the pack horses in his wake.

"Easy for you to talk, stranger," the man with the rippling muscles rasped in the same low tones.

The slitted eyes were fixed upon the rugged features of the youngster as the half-breed rode by him. "Sure is," he allowed. "My Ma taught me, real young. Later, my Pa taught me a few things."

There was no response to this beyond further futile words and the heavy silence of massed frustration followed the half-breed across the wooden bridge and on to the town's single street. Then a new sound impressed itself upon the lazy hum of the morning: the angry hiss of vented high pressure. This, in turn, was drowned by the rapid *thump-thump-thump* of a large piston. Grey vapor began to issue in short spurts from an outlet at the side of the lumber mill as a powerful steam engine was surged into action.

Although the sounds came from a static engine, they were almost identical to those made by a locomotive barrelling along a railroad; and as Edge dismounted in front of the church he could not prevent his memory from flipping forward a vivid series of recollections from the distant past. For the sound of hissing steam and pumping pistons inevitably flooded his mind with images of his escape from the Confederate hellhole of Andersonville* and the suffering that preceded it.† But then a harsher noise drove the past back where it belonged—the tortured sound of a fast-spinning saw blade ripping into a fresh log.

"Dear God, not more!"

* *See - Edge: Seven Out of Hell.*
† *See - The Blue, The Grey And The Red.*

78

Edge turned to look across at the side of the tiny church. The grave dug for Ezra Hyams had been filled and there were two more fresh mounds. The pot-bellied, pink-faced preacher was just unbending from fixing markers into position at the head of each new elongated heap. The painted letters, shiny in the sun, signalled the final resting places of Bradbury and Bucher.

"Where on earth am I going to bury them?" the man asked anxiously, spreading his hands to encompass the restricted cemetery between the church and the hotel. It was close packed with neat mounds, allowing just enough space to walk between them.

Edge nodded as he moved to one of the pack horses and delved a hand into the hip pocket of the deputy with the slit throat. "Seems you got yourself a grave problem, preacher," he drawled, pulling out a billfold.

"Hey, you!"

Edge glanced along the street and saw a short, powerfully-built man step from the doorway of the law office. A star set into a circle pinned to his vest pocket proclaimed his right to be there. Edge spat into the dust and returned his attention to the leather billfold. He flipped it open and saw a ten, a five and seven ones inside.

"You! I'm talking to you, mister!"

The lawman had a pompous voice. And his walk had more than a hint of the arrogant in it as he strutted angrily towards Edge.

"Preacher?"

"What do you want?" The man who sweated above the dog collar seemed genuinely concerned by the problem of where to bury the new dead:

and annoyed at the half-breed for causing the anxiety.

"Answer me, man!"

Edge sighed and looked at the town's new law. He was about forty and did not have the right kind of face to top off the ruggedly-formed body. It was round and deeply tanned, the flesh molded in pleasant lines and surfaced by smooth, unblemished skin. The green eyes were spaced close together and looked crafty. The wide mouth had a weak look above a chin that cut away towards the throat too soon. The black material of his vest was speckled with dandruff where it curved over the broad shoulders. He was hatless and didn't have a great deal of rust colored hair to keep the sun off his greasy skull. The circle around the star was inscribed with the message that he was a Montana Territorial Marshal. He wore a Trantor revolver high on each hip. Both guns had mother-of-pearl butt pieces. His vest, shirt, pants and boots looked expensive. But as the half-breed's hooded eyes met those of the lawman, the return stare warned against mistaking the marshal for a dude who happened to wear a star.

"I'm talking to you."

"Obliged if you wouldn't interrupt," Edge said easily, and swung his head to look back at the preacher. "How much a hat like this cost in Hate, feller?" he touched the brim of his hat.

Both the preacher and the marshal flinched at the name. The ten men rejected for work at the mill had crossed the bridge and stood watching with a subdued air of anticipation. Edge sensed other eyes upon him, hidden by the reflected glare

80

of sunlight on windows and the dark shadows of doorways.

"Town isn't called that," the preacher replied.

"Ain't what I asked." Edge could hear the rapid, angry breathing of the marshal.

The preacher sighed. "About a dollar, maybe. No more."

"Obliged," Edge told him, extracted a dollar and pushed the billfold back into the pocket of the dead deputy. Then he turned to the marshal and dropped his chin to his chest, showing the hole drilled through the brim of the hat at the back. "Feller did that before I killed him," he explained as he jerked up his head. "Man shouldn't go out owing folks."

The marshal forced his rage to stay below the surface. For just as Edge had recognized in him the signs of a man able to take care of himself, so the marshal had seen the far more blatant danger signals given off by the half-breed.

"You killed these men?" He sounded slightly incredulous.

"Two of 'em," Edge replied. "Self-defense. After one of 'em blasted the third guy."

"You think I'm about to believe that?"

Edge caught up the reins of his stolen gelding and set his mouth in a cruel line as his eyes glittered with ice cold anger. "You think I'd haul these stiffs back into town if I'd bush-whacked 'em?" he snarled.

He started to lead the horse towards the front of The Last Drop Hotel. The marshal hurried forward to examine the corpses, wrinkling his snub nose at the stink of them.

"Two of these men are deputies!" he yelled,

whirling to look across the street, his hands coming up and then dropping to curl around the fancy butts of the Trantors. But he did not draw the guns.

Edge hitched the horse to the rail in front of the hotel and turned slowly. His arms hung loosely at his sides, right hand inches from the Colt and left ready to snatch the Winchester from the boot. "Being a law officer don't guarantee a man a long life, marshal," he warned evenly. "You draw those cute irons, start blasting. Or don't ever point them at me again. Those two deputies got the same warning. But seems they were deaf as well as dumb."

The marshal had left his move too late, and he knew it. Edge was at the side of the street, close to the cover offered by the open double doors of the saloon. He was exposed in the center of the sunlit street. Hostile eyes were focused upon him from all directions and each thud of the piston through the cylinder seemed to drive home harder the mistake of making a play. Sweat beads stood out on his high forehead, then coursed downwards. He dropped his hands away from the guns.

"You haven't heard the last of this business, mister!" he challenged.

The words rang with the hollowness of an empty threat in his own ears and he whirled abruptly and stalked back towards the law office. Edge watched him halfway to his destination before swinging around and entering the saloon.

"That showed him, Mr. Edge!" Billy McNally called in delight as he turned from peering out into the street through a crack in the boards masking the broken window.

The moon face of the man with the mind of a child was wreathed in a beaming smile, far removed from the expression Edge had last seen on the smooth features.

"You've got no sense of direction, feller," Edge told him as he crossed the saloon towards the doorway which gave on to the restaurant.

"Sure I have!" Billy argued with feeling. "I was headed straight for Trasker when I run into that lousy marshal. He brung me back."

Cyrus McNally emerged from the doorway in back of the bar and eyed Edge with his normal apprehensiveness. "Anyone who knows Billy knows he ain't safe to be on his own, mister. Anytime they see him outside of town, they bring him back." He rested a closed fist on the bar top and when he opened it, loose change spilled out. "Billy, thanks you. I don't."

Edge's impassive gaze flicked from the father to the son. "Billy?" He held out the dollar bill he had taken from the dead deputy.

The simpleton's retarded mind slipped easily from depression to glee. "Yeah, Mr. Edge?"

"Please," the old man begged.

"No sweat," Edge told him, then to the son: "Go down to the store and buy me a hat. Same size, color and style as this one." He took off the hat and gave it into the eager hands along with the bill. "You get nothing for going but the walk."

Billy's mood did not alter. "That's okay, Mr. Edge. Ain't much reason to want to leave town when Marshal Colman's here. Ain't hardly any trouble when he's around. Corners and his help keep real quiet."

"Go buy the man his hat," the elder McNally snapped at the younger.

"Sure thing," Billy replied, and scuttled out of the door.

"Enough in that pile for breakfast?" Edge asked.

The old man poked the heap of change with a nervous finger. "More than."

Edge nodded that he wanted some food and dropped into a chair near the restaurant entrance, resting the Winchester across a table. "What's that marshal got over Corners, except rank?" he asked absently.

"I wouldn't know nothin' that ain't my business," the old man answered pointedly.

Edge curled back his lips into a grin as the bartender turned to shuffle through the doorway into the back. "Maybe it's just that Colman's pretty hot stuff," he muttered.

CHAPTER SIX

EDGE checked the restaurant and found it empty. He also saw that it had no direct entry or exit to either the front or rear of the building. So he elected to eat the breakfast of steak, grits and eggs at the table in the saloon. This placed him midway between the main front entrance and the doorway that gave on to the back of the premises behind the bar. He had half drunk his second cup of coffee when the new hat was delivered.

It was brought by a sallow-faced man of middle years with sandy-colored hair and frightened eyes of light brown. He was short and thin and had nervous, constantly moving hands dotted with freckles on their backs. He sidled rather than walked into the shade of the saloon from the bright splash of sunlight in the street—like a crab emerging from the sea.

"I fetched your hat, Mr. Edge," he said in a croaky voice as he halted in front of the table.

Edge nodded and took the hat. Apart from the ingrained dirt, stains and bullet hole of the old one, it was a perfect match. The half-breed tried it on and found the fit perfect.

"I'll put the word around."

"What?" The man blinked several times.

"Drum up some business for you," Edge answered. "Among guys with bullet holes in their hats. Dollar enough?"

"Dollar ten," the man rapped out automatically in store-keeper cadence. Then he blinked again and shook his head rapidly to remind himself that wasn't what he had come for.

"Preacher's taking care of a guy with his throat cut," Edge told him. "Better collect what's owed before a place's found to bury him."

The man swallowed hard. "I'm running a discount this week."

"Running scared, too," Edge said, fixing the storekeeper with a glinting scare. "You got something to say, better get it out fast, feller. Way you're sweating, likely to melt clean away soon."

"Maclean must have got to talk to you before he was killed, Mr. Edge." It was a statement rather than a question.

Edge nodded. "Didn't say a lot. No more than a thousand bucks. Hardly worth getting killed for—anybody getting killed."

The storekeeper took out a large, damp handkerchief and made it wetter as he mopped his face. "All we can afford, Mr. Edge." A fragile smile lit his sallow features. "But you came back to Corn. . . . Hate." He sounded very pleased to speak the forbidden name. Then he glanced around nervously, wringing his hands together. They were alone except for Cyrus McNally who was dusting off unused glasses behind the bar.

"I came back to sort out another matter," the half-breed replied, and finished the coffee. He curled back his thin lips to expose his even teeth in a grin. "but it may be we're interested in the same thing, feller."

The man blinked. "Oh?" He cleared his throat. "What do you want us to do, Mr. Edge?"

"Take up the collection," the half-breed replied.

The man's smile was brighter this time, but still very vulnerable to an attack of nerves. Even Edge's steady gaze was a threat, so the man swung away and moved quickly to the bar. "You wanna kick in to start it, Cyrus?" he asked.

The old bartender did so, with slow reluctance. He gave a nod, shuffled out into the back and returned a few moments later with a bundle of crinkled bills. He eyed the money ruefully for stretched seconds, then handed the ill-used bills to the storekeeper: like a man investing his life-savings in an operation in which he had no faith.

"Thanks, Mr. Edge," the storekeeper called, and hurried out.

The half-breed took out the makings and rolled a cigarette. He lit it, then split the match and used the pointed end for a tooth-pick.

"What am I supposed to do to earn it?" he asked to end a long silence in the stuffy saloon.

A million dust motes began to float smoothly again in the sunlight shafting through the open doorway, settling down after the agitation of the storekeeper's exit.

"You must know," McNally accused dully, returning to the chore of cleaning the glasses.

"Got to be one thing or another," Edge allowed. "Either run Corners out of Hate or kill him."

"Corners won't let anybody run him out."

Edge nodded through the smoke from his cigarette. "And I won't let anybody hire me to kill somebody," he said softly.

The regular series of sounds from the steam engine at the mill were infiltrated by other noises—

from the side of the hotel. Shovels being thrust into the ground to dig up clods of earth.

"So Alex Burgess is wasting his time collecting up that money," McNally muttered.

"Didn't say that," Edge corrected. "Could be I'll have to kill Corners to settle my beef with him. In that case I wouldn't be averse to taking the thousand."

"Strange way of thinking," McNally said flatly.

"Maybe it's the town that's affecting me," the half-breed replied. "It's a strange place."

"Wasn't always the way it is now," McNally said, a trifle heatedly.

"Nothing is," Edge answered. "It's called progress. Ain't always good."

Running footfalls sounded out on the street and the old man's son lumbered into the saloon, breathless and sweating.

"They're comin', Pa!" he panted. "Miss Dorrie and some men. I counted six of 'em!"

Edge crushed out the cigarette in the drying grease on his plate.

"Billy's talking about the gunslingers Corners sent to Trasker for," the old man explained. "He wanted to send one of his deputies for them. But his bitch of a niece said she'd go. Reckoned she wanted to do something to help get you, mister."

"Guess I must have upset her a little," Edge understated.

"Way out still," Billy cut in. "Ridin' slow. Reckon me and the others'll have the graves dug before they get here."

"Preacher found some space then?" Edge asked.

"Openin' up old graves," the simpleton answered. "It was my idea." He grinned. "Makes the diggin' easier." He turned and hurried out.

"Like I said before, that feller ain't so simple," Edge told his father.

"Thea used to be a good town to live in," the old man continued, picking up from where Billy had interrupted the conversation. "This place was mine. Storekeepers owned their own places. The lumber men worked their own areas of timber. Had to haul the trees whole to Trasker, but it worked okay. Then Corners moved in and built the mill." He shrugged his thin shoulders. "Nobody was about to raise any objections. Lot easier to just haul the trees down to the mill, get paid and let Corners worry about freighting out the milled planks."

"Acted the nice guy in those days?" Edge said, feeling pleasantly drowsy from the effects of the heat and the food.

"Like his middle name was kindness," McNally replied sourly. "Had a lot of it to spread around. The dollar kind. Opened up the bank next door and started to lend out money." His tone became more bitter. "My boy's the town idiot, mister. But turned out we was all simple enough to get took by Luke Corners. Got everyone in town in debt to his bank, then foreclosed. Me and the rest of the folk in business had to sell to him to pay back the debts. Lumber men had to start working for him instead of themselves or be tossed out of their homes."

"Nobody objected then, either?"

McNally banged a glass on the bar top, so hard it shattered. He cursed. "Not a thing we could do about it. Corners had the territorial law on his side. Marshal Colman came to town and told us that. In three-and-a-half years, Corners got to own this town—lock, stock and barrel. And he had the papers to prove it."

"And nobody left?"

"Couple of youngsters with no kin or responsibilities. Corners let us keep our houses and businesses, rented from him. Takes a lot for a man to uproot himself and his family from the place he's sweated his guts out to build up." McNally gave another shrug of his emaciated shoulders. "Guess everybody just kept hopin' a feller like you'd come ridin' through. Never did happen 'til now, though. Corners changed the town name, made himself sheriff and judge, and brung in gunsels to call deputies."

"How about Colman?" Edge asked, standing up and stretching, flexing his muscles to drive out the threat of inertia.

McNally used one of his cupped hands to scrape the broken glass into an ashpan. "Nothin' but a shit," he said vehemently. "Rides in twice, maybe three times a year. Inspection tour, he calls it. Lumber man tried to tell him what was happenin' one time. Coleman listened to him, but didn't do nothin' except tell Corners. Day after Colman left, lumber man had an accident. Fell under a loaded wagon out back of the mill. Marshal's on a kickback, mister. Long as Corners don't cause no trouble while he's here, Colman turns in a good report."

Edge moved to the doorway and scanned the street. It was empty, except for the two dogs stretched out under the water trough. The horse he had ridden and the three which had carried the dead men had been led away into the shade somewhere. He guessed Billy had attended to the chore. The sounds of the grave digging continued to come from around the side of the hotel. He saw a movement down at the far end of the street, and recognized the stooped form of Alex Burgess emerge from one house and scuttle into another.

"Corners lets you run a Citizens Committee," the half-breed said as he swung his head to look in the other direction—out across the bridge, past the lumber mill and along the trail.

"With one of his deputies sittin' in," McNally replied bitterly.

Three flatbed wagons were stalled halfway to the trees. A group of riders were clustered around the lead wagon. As Edge watched, the horsemen urged their mounts into a gallop, heading for town. Dust billowed behind them. The wagons lurched into a tight turn and the teams were whipped into pursuit of the riders.

"Not last night," Edge said, turning from the door to cross towards the foot of the stairway.

"Secret meetin'," McNally replied.

"A deputy found out what was said at the meeting," the half-breed revealed, and held out a hand. "Obliged if I could have my old room back."

Anger and confusion did battle across the old man's thin features. He reached under the bar, hauled out a key and arced it across the saloon. Edge caught it.

"We got a spy!" McNally rasped.

"Reckon so," Edge replied as he started up the stairs. "Ought to be Burgess or Maclean, but I guess it ain't. Got a guy named Philby in town?"

"No," the old man answered, perplexed.

"Just a thought," Edge called as he went from sight on to the landing.

As he moved along to the door at the end, galloping hoofbeats sounded out on the trail, clattered over the bridge and along the street. The riders reined their horses to a skidding halt outside the hotel and, as Edge slid the key into the lock, boots scraped against the floorboards of the saloon.

"Six beers, bartender!" a man demanded raucously. "Ridin's thirsty work in this heat."

Edge swung open the door as, down in the saloon voices were raised in agreement with the opening remark.

"Ease in slow and set that rifle down gentle," Marshal Colman instructed the half-breed.

Edge remained frozen in the doorway for stretched seconds, hooded eyes cold and lips set in a thin, cruel line. The stockily-built lawman was sitting on the side of the bed, pointing both his revolvers at the tall half-breed. The hands folded around the ornate butts of the guns were as steady as Edge's gaze.

"Hurry it up, old-timer!" a man roared below. "I been eating dust most of the night."

"Said out there on the street wouldn't be the last of it," the marshal said as Edge stepped across the threshold and closed the door behind him. "The rifle, mister."

"Should have believed you," Edge replied, leaning the Winchester against the wall at the side of the door. "Real smart of you to get into my room."

"I make out," the lawman said, easing up from the bed.

"Yeah, you're a keen as mustard, Colman."

"You're under arrest. Unbuckle the gunbelt."

Edge began to comply. "How'd you get in here?" he asked evenly.

The marshal refused to be captured by the half-breed's steady gaze. Instead, he concentrated upon the long brown fingers as they unfastened the belt buckle. "Bill McNally will do anything for a handful of pennies. I bought your room number and his pass key."

Edge nodded. "Guess he'll be heading out for Trasker again," he said, allowing the gunbelt and holstered Colt to thud to the floor.

"Way it ought to be," Colman answered. "Impressionable man like he is shouldn't be forced to watch too many hangings. I'm taking you across the street to stand trial."

"For what?" Edge asked.

"Record will show murder—of those three men you hauled into town." The weak-looking face of the lawman was abruptly twisted out of shape by venomous thoughts.

"But I'll know it's for making me look a fool out there awhile ago."

"Have to plead guilty to that," the half-breed admitted easily, and the casual words lit fires of rage in the dark eyes.

But Colman controlled himself in an instant. It was further proof that the man was no fool: knew better than to allow a prisoner to taunt him into anger. An angry man does not think rationally and is therefore prone to make errors. Possibly a fatal error in this situation. So the marshal forced himself to be coldly calm: and died anyway.

"Turn around and open the door!" he rasped.

He stepped away from the bed and in front of the window. Edge saw the flash of sunlight on gun

93

metal and the figure of a man crouched on the roof of the courthouse across the street. "Ain't been nice knowing you, marshal," Edge said softly, and waited for the tell-tale puff of muzzle smoke.

The crack of the shot sounded a split-second later, merging with the smash of splintered glass. In that instant, Colman expressed bewilderment at the half-breed's comment. Then Edge powered down into a crouch and the marshal's puzzlement was frozen into a death mask. The bullet took him midway up his back, to the side of his spine. It tunnelled through his flesh, smashed chips from a rib bone and sank deep into his heart. It didn't exit.

Edge had the Winchester in his hands as Colman started to fall forward, arms dropping limply to his sides and matched Trantors clunking to the floor. The dead man crashed on top of them. An expanding stain of dark red spread across the back of his expensive vest.

"I got him!" the man on the courthouse roof yelled ecstatically as flies droned in through the smashed window and swarmed around the fresh blood.

Edge crossed the room in a crouch, slitted eyes directed at the sharpshooter who was on his feet, dancing a gleeful jig. The flies swooped away as a bone cracked. It was a bone in Colman's hand as the half-breed's unmindful heel crunched down. The marshal did not feel it—and the man on the courthouse roof did not hear it. Neither did he hear the metallic clicks as Edge worked the Winchester's lever action to pump a shell into the breech. He probably heard the explosion of the bullet from the muzzle.

He was hit in the face, the lead smashing into

him below the nostrils. It tore a furrow across the down on to the roof of the courthouse with no roof of his mouth and tunnelled through his head to burst free at the back of his neck. The bullet killed him as he was in mid-air, completing a small jump in his crazy dance routine. He smacked hard down on to the roof of the courthouse with no muscles to hold him erect. His legs buckled and he executed an almost graceful spiral as his body collapsed. Blood spouted from the entry and exit holes of the bullet, inscribing ugly splashes of red across the sparkling white façade of the building. Then he toppled over the eaves.

Only now did a scream pierce the hot air. But it did not emerge from the blood-run mouth of the dead man. It was high and female, uttered by Dorrie Corners as the dead weight of the falling corpse smashed on top of her and crushed her to the courthouse steps.

Edge caught a fleeting glimpse of the woman a moment before she was knocked down. Frozen in an attitude that was half-relaxed , half-terrified Dressed in black blouse and pants with her hair rolled up under a grey hat. Her clothing was dusty from the ride. So was the pad of dressing that covered the bullet wound on her cheek. The unmasked parts of her face and the posture of her body beneath the tight-fitting clothes suggested fear. But the way she rested a rolled parasol on the steps was a clue to the casual way in which she had been waiting for the fatal shot to be fired.

Now, as she recovered from the horror, she struggled desperately to wriggle out from under the corpse. Edge waited until she had got her head and shoulders out from under, then thrust the Win-

95

chester forward. The muzzle struck a shard of glass still held in the window frame. It was smashed free and the sound froze the woman's struggles. Her wide eyes were fastened upon the figure of Edge standing at the window, aiming the rifle at her. She groaned.

"Sometimes things just get on top of you, don't they?" the half-breed called wryly.

CHAPTER SEVEN

THE regular hiss and thump of the steam engine that had been masked only fleetingly by the two shots, was at once doing battle with the rattle and hoofbeats of the wagons approaching at high speed. The engine noises lost out for awhile when the wagons reached the end of the trail. Edge leaned out through the window and snapped a glance towards the source of the sound. He saw the first two wagons make a dust billowing turn in through the gateway of the lumber mill as the third one skidded and swayed to a halt on ths bridge. He had time to spot Corners as the passenger and the squint-eyed deputy as driver before he flicked his slitted eyes back to the woman. She had not moved, pinned down by the physical weight of the corpse and the mental pressure of the pointing Winchester.

"Uncle Luke!" she yelled.

"You stupid fools!" the big, silver-haired man bellowed.

"Corners!" Edge shouted as a floorboard out on the landing creaked.

"Let her up, you bastard!"

"Call you hired guns out of the saloon!" Edge shouted back. Another creak out on the landing. He poised his muscles. "I figure five."

"You let Dorrie up and then I'll—"

The half-breed was not listening. His ears were

97

strained to pick up sounds from behind him. He heard the faint scratch of the metal tongue withdrawing from the groove as the door handle was turned.

"Correction!" he shouted, and whirled. He jerked the Winchester in from the window and swung it. The door was cracking open. He fired, pumped, fired, pumped, fired, pumped. A splintered hole in the left of the door, another in the right and a third in the center. The first and second hit the man. In the chest and throat. He was flying backwards by the impact of the bullets, dying with a gasp. He hit the wall hard, and crashed forward. His forehead cracked against the unlatched door and flung it open. He stretched across the threshold and was still. The flies did a meal hop from the marshal to the gunslinger.

"Make that four!" the half-breed called as he swung back to the window.

Dorrie had struggled another few inches clear, but the menace of the rifle froze her again. Corners was halted abruptly, too. He had leapt from the wagon, shotgun at the ready. But he had made only a couple of yards from the bridge.

"What are you gonna do, drifter?" the big man snarled. Sweat beads ran down his mis-shapen nose and splashed into the dust.

"Kill her in five seconds—and I ain't counting out loud."

"Come on outta there!" Corners roared frantically. More splashes in the dust: this time from spittle that spilled from each side of his mouth and made the long drop from his quivering jaw.

Between the thud of the piston and the hiss of steam, boot leather scraped on the floorboards of the saloon. Edge dropped his gaze and saw the four men move out into the sunlight as a group.

"He's bluffing, Mr. Corners," one of them drawled. "Took us longer than five seconds to come out."

Two of them still held glasses of beer. They sipped from them as they ambled across to where Corners stood.

"Never was much at telling the time," Edge responded. "But I sure as hell can shoot good."

"That ain't no lie," the talkative gunslinger agreed with a rueful glance at the dead man draped over Dorrie. "Always thought Jake could as well."

The four were of a type. Hard-faced, solidly-built: lithe bodies constantly primed for action and glinting eyes for ever alert to signs that action was required. And more than this. The indefinable mark that violent death could well be the result of the action. The killer type. Edge's type.

"He could," the half-breed assured the spokesman.

"Who'd he blast?" the man wanted to know, and took a swig of his beer.

"Nobody important. A crooked territorial marshal."

All four grinned, but it was the same man who change took place. Once or twice his broad mouth you. Weren't no reward on him."

Corners was fuming with silent anger as the exchange took place. Once or twice his broad mouth flapped open, but no words were uttered.

"Guess you killed Bob as well?" He spoke in the tone of one asking another whether he had read the paper that morning.

99

"Reckon so. He fell down and he ain't got up yet."

The man finished his beer and nodded as he ran the back of his hand across his lips. "No sweat, mister. Just cuts down the competition for that five grand Mr. Corners here has put up."

"Uncle Luke!" Dorrie pleaded with a note of hysteria adding a shriek to her voice.

"I told you to play it cool!" Corners bellowed, finding his voice at last. "I told you to wait 'til Colman left town."

Three of the men seemed about to whirl on Corners: perhaps even gun him down for his criticism. But their spokesman spread an incongruous expression of pained innocence across his rugged, deeply burnished features. "Hell, Mr. Corners," he defended in a fake tone to match the phoney expression. "Weren't any of us that tried to blast the drifter. It was Jake and Bob."

"And look what happened to them," Edge warned easily.

"We come outta the saloon like you wanted," the garrulous gunman went on. "And that's real hard to do on a hot day like it is."

Corners' piercing eyes shifted from the men he had hired, to his niece, then up to the window where Edge stood. "What now?" he barked, almost in complete control of his rage.

It would have been as easy as swinging the Winchester and squeezing the trigger to kill Corners. But he was not fooled by the easy attitudes of the hired guns who stood calmly beside their boss. Not one casually swinging gun hand was more than six inches from the butt of a Colt jutting from a tied-down holster. With the big man dead, there would be no five grand reward. But spite can be a force as powerful as greed. Which was a consideration Edge may have taken into account when Corners was a sitting target on the wagon. That and the fact that he could expect no help from the citizens of Hate. The street was deserted except for the five men and the trapped woman. And although only one deputy was left with the men at the mill, there was no sound or sign of a revolt from that direction.

"Back off over the bridge with the Trasker guns," the half-breed responded to Corners' query.

"What about Dorrie?" the big man demanded.

"Reckon she'll be happy to stay," Edge told him, flicking his eyes away from the men to the woman, and back again. The rifle continued to draw a bead on her terrified face. "Seeing as how she got knocked off her feet by the man there."

Corners seemed about to hurl a challenge up at Edge, but abruptly he thought better of it. He whirled and strode angrily back towards the bridge, barking an order to the deputy aboard the wagon."

"Uncle Luke!" Dorrie wailed plaintively.

The deputy jumped down from the seat and began to tug on the bridles of the two horses to back them across the bridge.

"Be seein' you feller," the spokesman for the quartet of bounty hunters called. "Next time without a gun in your hand."

He led the men in the wake of Corners. As the wagon was backed clear of the bridge, allowing Corners and the gunslingers to cross, Edge hooked a leg over the jagged glass of the smashed window and found a foothold on a narrow ledge that ran along the façade of the hotel. He flattened his body against the wall at the side of the window, hooked out his other leg, then jumped. Dust billowed from beneath his thudding feet. He landed in a bent-knee crouch and jerked erect immediately, snapping the rifle back to the aim at the trapped woman. From the hip now.

"Why didn't you break a leg!" Dorrie groaned.

Edge's lip curled back to show the cold grin. "I seen you twice in two days, Miss Dorrie," he drawled. "Man's just gotta have some good luck to balance the bad."

"Bastard!" she rasped as Edge crossed the street towards her and two splashes sounded from the river.

The half-breed halted close to the woman and looked across the bridge as he lowered the rifle to rest the muzzle on the nape of Dorrie's neck. The two gunslingers who had brought their beers out of the saloon had ditched the empty glasses into the river. Now, as Corners spoke rapidly to the men at his heels, they moved as a tightknit group through the open gates. Once on the lumber mill property, the gunslingers snatched out their Colts. The deputy levelled his Winchester and Corners swung up the double-barrelled shotgun. Every weapon was aimed at the group of twenty-five lumber men who had been standing in sweating silence between the two parked wagons since the first rifle shot had cracked out. The second deputy emerged from the mill and moved quickly across to align himself with his partner. His Winchester was as menacing as the other guns as it was trained upon the lumber men. The steam engine thudded home its piston twice more and died with a hiss of escaping vapor. One of the dogs barked and sniffed at the tension

102

taut air: decided it was too hot to investigate further and sunk its head back into the dust to sleep. Flies droned and the water wheel churned.

"Let Dorrie loose or we gun down these men!" Corners yelled, looking back over his shoulder, through the wire mesh fencing, over the river and along the street.

The big man was at least three hundred feet away, but his words rang out clearly. Distinct enough for Edge to catch the note of triumph in his tone. The woman with the gun in her neck was also able to inject a hint of scornful victory in her voice.

"Looks like Lady Luck ran out on you again, you lousy skunk!" she hissed through lips forced down hard against the step.

"You hear me, drifter?" Corners yelled.

Edge spat, the globule of moisture hitting the cement close to the woman's head. "Loud and clear!" he called back.

"So do it!"

"Loud and clear, but you ain't making no sense!" the half-breed responded.

"Twenty-five men, drifter."

He was still looking back over his shoulder, evil joy registered on his rugged features.

"One woman!" Edge called pointedly.

Corners' happiness evaporated like the final threads of steam sucked into nothingness by the fierce sun. From thinking of himself on the brink of victory, Corners suddenly faced defeat. His complexion seemed abruptly more dark in comparison wth his silver hair. The attitudes of the men arrayed helplessly before the guns did not alter. They appeared as docile animals, moulded to accept the wishes of their masters. Yet each one had a revolver in his holster.

"You must figure a deal of some kind!" Corners snarled.

"You for her!" the half-breed called.

The big man shook with a spasm of fury, and it was deep-seated enough to again curtail his ability to speak.

"No deal there, feller!" the talkative gunslinger inserted into the pause. "Blast the dame and no sweat. But you cream Corners—why, me or one of my buddies is out five grand. Make us mad. Mad enough to gun down these men just for the hell of it."

Edge sighed. "They ain't men and being dead's probably perferable to living in Hate." He turned to look down at the back of the woman's head against which the rifle muzzle rested. "When you get to hell keep the welcome warm for Uncle Luke," he raspe.

"No!"

The single word had the impact of a rifle shot in the instant of silence that followed the half-breed's low-keyed words. It came from much closer than the far side of the river. And trembled against the hot, bright air with much greater meance than any threat Corners or the gunslinger had voiced. Edge had his back turned to the open doorway of the saloon. A tiny bead of sweat erupted from a pore beneath the soft leather of the razor pouch and coursed down the ridged skin covering his spine. It left a cold trail on his flesh and he knew a gun was trained upon him. The Winchester stayed pressing into the back of Dorrie's neck beneath the brim of her

104

crushed hat. Edge turned his head slowly to look over his shoulder.

Cyrus McNally did not look frail anymore. There was the strength of determined intent in his emaciated face, with resolution shining from his sunken eyes. He held the half-breed's own Colt in a two-handed grip, thrust out in front of him to the full-length of his arms. The hands were rock steady and the curled trigger finger showed a white knuckle.

"You want something, feller?" Edge asked, his tone as ice cold as the glinting-eyed gaze he fixed upon McNally.

But the old man was not provoked into fear. The lost opportunities of a lifetime seemed to have built up inside his slight physique: become concentrated into a powerful force that numbed his nerve into non-existence. For him it was all or nothing.

"Twenty-five lives is too high a price to pay," McNally replied.

The men across the river were too far away to hear the exchange of conversation after the first word had exploded from McNally's bloodness lips. They waited in the blazing heat, like motionless replicas cast in stone: stone that sweated.

"I agree!"

Edge swung his head to look over the other shoulder. The pink-faced preacher was framed in the doorway of his tiny church. Movement, not sound, drew the half-breed's attention to other citizens of Hate. They emerged from the houses and stores. Ten men—the stooped old one wearing a pad of white dressing on his head wound—many more woman and a clutch of children. They formed into a three-deep line and advanced slowly down the street, dragging their feet in the dust: like a sloppy military unit. They said nothing, but their expressions told all.

"Reckon I have to bow to the wishes of the silent majority," Edge said evenly, and stepped to the side, taking the rifle muzzle away from the woman's neck. It left an angry red ring on the white flesh just below the hairline.

He sloped the Winchester casually across his shoulder and swung around easily to lean his back against the courthouse wall. The Colt in the double-handed grip moved fractionally to keep him covered. Fear had drained Dorrie of her final reserve of strength and her struggles were pathetically inadequate as the weight of the dead man bore down upon her.

"Help me?" she pleaded, craning her neck around to look up at Edge.

"Your problem's outta my hands now," the half-breed replied quietly. "Up to somebody else to get you out from under."

CHAPTER EIGHT

"MCNALLY?"

"Yes, Mr. Corners!" the bartender shouted back.

"You got the drop on the drifter?"

"Yes, Mr. Corners!"

A Colt revolver across a range of a street's width was not an accurate weapon. Particularly if the target was on the move. But the half-breed remained casually leaning against the white-painted frame

"No deal here, feller!" the talkative gunslinger frontage of the courthouse, unwilling to put McNally's disadvantage to the test.

"Then let Dorrie go or we'll kill these men!" Corners yelled.

"I'd thank you to wait awhile," McNally replied, sunken eyes and Colt still trained upon Edge.

"Uncle Luke!" Dorrie called, but her voice was as weakened by tension as her physical strength.

Corners gave no indication that he had heard the simple plea. "For what?" he roared.

"Situation ain't changed, Mr. Corners. We still both got somethin' the other wants."

"So we have to trust each other!" the big man with the shotgun countered. "Soon as my niece steps on to the bridge, I'll turn the men loose."

Some of the hardness drained away from McNally's face. Something akin to anguish replaced it as he forced his mind to examine the offer.

"No deal!" one of the men among the bystanders

rapped out, and stepped from the group. The other nine followed him. As they moved across the line of fire between McNally and Edge, the half-breed had the perfect opportunity to take command of the situation again.

Instead, he rested the Winchester against the wall beside him and dug into his shirt pocket for the makings. As he started to roll the cigarette, five of the men drew rifles from the boots hung on the saddles of the gunslingers' horses, which were still hitched to the rail in front of the hotel. The sixth rifle was up on the courthouse roof. Two men crossed the street toward Edge, ignoring him as he struck a match and lit his cigarette. Hope shone in the woman's eyes as one of the men stooped over her. But he simply jerked the revolver out of the dead man's holster. His companion went into the courthouse on the trail of the discarded rifle. "Thanks for nothing!" the woman hissed.

The man with the revolver showed her a hateful sneer. "Nothin's all you'll ever get from me, bitch!" he rasped, and spat into her upturned face.

She groaned.

"What's happening?" Corners roared. "McNally? I'll kill them for sure!"

The three lumber men still without stolen guns eyed the Colt in the old man's hands. Then realization hit them and they went into the hotel on the run.

"McNally told you to wait, Corners!"

The harsh words were yelled by the man who was stripped to the waist. He stood in the center of the street with his rifle, like those of the other men, aimed from the hip across the river.

108

"You'll all . . .," Corners began, then bit back the threat. "Call it, Laine. But be damn careful."

Laine ignored him.

"We got your two brothers and your old man in front of these guns."

Laine's handsome face did not alter its expression of cool calm as he turned toward Edge. "Can we trust you not to interfere, mister?" he asked.

There was a scraping noise from the roof of the courthouse as the man found the rifle and crouched down. A man appeared at the broken window of Edge's room in the hotel. He had one of Colman's fancy revolvers. Two other men appeared at two other windows. One had the mate of the marshal's gun: the other cocked the dead gunslinger's Remington.

"Answer me a question," Edge asked through a cloud of cigarette smoke.

"Yeah?" Laine responded.

"They toy guns in your holsters?"

"Good as. Corners lets us keep 'em. But ain't no place in town to buy shells."

It explained the seemingly moronic docility of the lumber men arrayed before the mill. This, and the long years of hopeless obedience to the big man and his hired hands.

"Ain't one to spoil a good play," Edge said.

Laine considered this for a series of long moments, staring hard into the impassive face of the half-breed. He spoke to McNally while still looking into the glittering slits of light blue that gave nothing away.

"Relax, Cyrus. You did your bit."

The old man held his straight arm pose for a moment more, then lowered the gun. His body sagged against the doorframe and he was once more weak, defenseless and older than his years.

"We owe you, mister," Laine told Edge. "Whatever happens, we owe you. But . . ."

He let the opening word of the threat hang in the air.

"Laine!" Corners roared.

"I get the message," Edge replied softly, then leaned slightly to the side to look along the row of men at McNally. He raised his voice. "You did it once, feller," he called.

"What?" The voice was as empty of force as the thin body.

"Pointed a gun at me," the half-breed warned.

"Be with you in a couple of minutes!" Laine yelled to the impatient Corners. Then he turned to look back at the women. "Get your kids inside. Rest of you ladies help his bitch of a niece." He pointed the rifle into the space between the hotel and the bank. "And move her down the alley."

The mothers seemed disappointed that they had to withdraw from the center of the drama as they shepherded their unwilling children back into the houses. Dorrie caught her breath and held it in terror as the remainder of the women advanced upon her. They were smiling and the expressions looked out-of-place on their careworn faces.

"You men get down here!" Laine yelled to those at the hotel windows. He swung around to look up at the court house roof. "Larry, you let me know anything bad that happens over the river."

"Sure will," the man on the roof replied happily.

"No!" Dorrie moaned.

Two women—middle-aged and overweight, looking tougher than some of the lumber men—moved ahead of the group and stooped down at each side of the helpless Dorrie.

"Ain't gonna hurt you, dear," one of them placated.

"Not much, anyway," the second augmented.

Their big hands fixed like vices under Dorrie's armpits and jerked at her. She screamed softly as she was dragged out from under the dead weight and stood on her feet. Had the two women not supported her, her legs would have collapsed.

Laine was speaking in low tones to the other women, and their smiles brightened as they listened. They crowded around Dorrie and her captors and moved as a close-knit group across the street and into the alley where the gallows stood. Laine spoke with the other lumber men and they followed the women.

"What are you doing with her?" Corners roared, his rage brushing hysteria to put a high-pitched shrieking note in his words.

"You'll see!" Laine snarled.

Edge dropped his cigarette and trod on it. He picked up the Winchester slowly, but not furtively, and canted it across his shouldar. His pace was casual and his expression disinterested as he moved over to the hotel entrance where McNally still sagged against the doorframe.

"I had to do it, Mr. Edge," the old man groaned, running a damp bandana around his throat to wipe away the sweat. "Hold that gun on you, I mean."

The half-breed nodded impassively and plucked the Colt from the loose-fingered hand. "Anyone can get to do it once," he allowed, and brushed past the old man to enter the saloon.

As always, the stale heat inside was as uncomfortable as the blazing sunlight outside. But the shade offered a pretense of coolness enjoyed by the mind if not the body. He went across to the bar, scooping up his gunbelt from a table as he went by. He had it on, with the Colt back in the holster by the time he reached the gap in the counter- and went through. McNally had taken the price of the breakfast from the pile of loose change. Edge separated another ten cents and drew himself a beer.

"Tell me something, mister?" McNally asked from the doorway.

Edge sipped the tepid beer.

"Would you really have shot Dorrie Corners? Got all those men killed?"

Edge finished the beer at a swallow, drew another and slid a further ten cents out of the pile of loose change as he headed back for the gap in the counter.

"Something neither of us will ever know now," he replied as he strolled toward the doorway.

"Laine, my patience is about run out!" Corners challenged. His tone altered abruptly. "What the hell?"

As Edge reached the doorway, he was in time to see eight men hauling on two lengths of rope, the strain of the weight they were pulling erupting great beads of sweat from every pore on each of their faces. Then, into view from out of the alley, came the platform with the grotesque gallows growing on top. Dorrie Corners—stark naked except for a bandana gag over her mouth and ropes lashing her ankles together and hands behind her back—stood with her head in the noose. The two

112

stoutly-built women flanked her, pressing a revolver into the soft flesh beneath each of her ears.

"Laine, I'll . . ."

Once more a glimmer of the rational fought through the turmoil of the big man's rage and he realized the hollowness of the threat he had been about to hurl.

"Women's idea to strip her!" Laine shouted, loud but flat.

"Ain't just to shame her," one of the female captors explained. "She always been a brazen huzzy. It's so you won't take too long making up your mind, Mr. Corners."

The platform was rested in the center of the street. Dorrie was positioned under the cross-strut of the gallows so that she was face-forward to the bridge. The gunslingers and deputies turned to gape at her nakedness: lustfully. The lumber men who were captives did not move, but an aura of hope rather than dejection hung above them now.

"She has to stay too long out in this sun," the second female captor called. "Could be she'll die of heatstroke before we can hang her."

Dorrie was forced to pivot slowly, presenting every facet of her naked body to each watching eye. The white skin seemed almost translucent but the strong, firm curves of breasts, belly, hips and thighs did not suggest frailness. Despite the terror visible in the twisted face with the screwed-shut eyes above the biting gag, the body advertised blatant sexuality. The women stared at the richly female flesh with envious contempt. Male eyes showed a range of expressions from rage to indifference. But it was lust that was uppermost, seeming to tremble in the stifling hot air.

Not until she had completed her enforced pivot did anybody else move. Then the men who had hauled the platform from the alley unfastened the ropes, hitched them together and tied one end to the trapdoor lever. The slack was fed out along the street behind the platform and the men and women moved forward to form a line. They picked up the rope. Only Edge, McNally and the preacher did not take a position in the line. Dorrie stood alone and trembling up on the platform, fighting to keep strength in her naked body in order to retain the slack in the noose.

"This is madness!" Corners shrieked.

"This is the way it's got to be," Laine called back coldly.

"Set those men free. Soon as the last one's back behind the gallows, I'll release your niece."

The spokesman for the hired guns spat. "Makes trusting a one-way thing," he drawled.

"Ain't a single soul on this line has ever killed anybody," Laine countered flatly. "Happy to keep it that way. Reckon you boys have a fair score between you. Makes us folks the most trustworthy."

There were long moments of silence, broken only by the churning water wheel. Then Dorrie gave a strangled groan through the gag.

"Turn them loose!" Corners barked abruptly. Spittle splashed from his jaw into the dust.

The two deputies lowered their rifles as three of the gunslingers tore their stares away from the nude woman to look at their spokesman.

"Standing here ain't earning me no five grand," he said reflectively, and fluidly slid his revolver into its holster. The others followed suit. "On your

114

way, guys," he told the lumber men. "No hard feelings, uh?"

"I got one," another of the gunmen muttered with a grin as he rubbed the bulge at the front of his pants.

"Shut your filthy mouth!" Corners snarled at him as the freed prisoners began to file through the gateway and across the bridge.

Not one of them looked up at the naked woman as they shuffled past her exposed sexuality. Each face was drenched with sweat and each shirt was plastered to the body by staining moisture. Not until he was behind the gallows platform, relatively safe from the guns across the river, did each man show his relief. When the last one had achieved this, Laine dropped the rope. Those in line behind him did the same, some of the women rushing forward to embrace their menfolk released from captivity.

Laine went forward and climbed up the steps to the platform. He drew a knife and suddenly the seven guns behind the lumber mill fence swung towards him. Coolly, the self-appointed leader of the revolt sliced through the ropes binding Dorrie's wrists and ankles. He did not have time to lift the noose clear of her head. She did that herself, then lunged forward, leaping down from the platform. Her bare feet slapped on the planking of the bridge in a panicked run. Her fingers worked frantically at the knot in the gag and when she dragged the constricting length of material clear, an animalistic scream was vented from her mouth. It maintained the same awful volume and pitch until she had streaked across the front of the mill and plunged into the merciful cover of the doorway.

There was somethnng eerily awe-inspiring about the woman's flight and the wailing that accompanied it. So that for the time it took to complete, the watchers were held transfixed, moving only their heads to follow the headlong progress of the nude Dorrie Corners. But then her uncle shook free of the sensation that all the world except for Dorrie had stood still. He vented his pent-up rage by jerking both triggers of the double-barrelled shotgun.

The scattering loads ripped a great, gaping hole in the fence and spouted a thousand white spumes from the surface of the river. But the twin explosions served as a signal and the gunslingers drew. A hail of bullets from their fanned revolvers sprayed into the street. But Laine had leapt clear of the gallows platform and the handguns were ineffective beyond this point. The Winchesters of the deputies were a different proposition—but both lawmen selected the same target.

The rifleman on the courthouse roof took a bullet in each shoulder. The impact of the twin bolts of lead flung him backwards from his crouch. As men and women in the street scuttled for cover, the man on the roof bounced against a chimney stack and was powered into a staggering, involuntary run. His leading foot plunged over the gutter and he tipped toward the ground. He screamed, then died, the top of his head impacting with the cement step. His skull cracked open and a pulpy mass of red, white and grey oozed from the ghastly split as his twitching body stretched out beside the inert form of the gunslinger.

Rifle and revolver fire spat viciously from doorways and the angles of buildings: sending the seven men beyond the fence scampering for the mill entrance which moments before had hidden Dorrie Corners' shame.

Edge and Cyrus McNally had ducked back into the hotel doorway when the double-barrelled shotgun exploded. Now the half-breed sucked the final heeltap of tepid foam from the bottom of the glass; as the old man stared in horror across the street at the newly dead Larry spilling out his brains on to the courthouse steps.

"That was Randy Cannons' boy," McNally said with infinite sadness as the firing stopped. "Randy was killed by one of Mr. Corners' deputies after some trouble. Now Larry's gone in the same way."

Blood from the massive wound in the dead man's head ran off the step and cascaded down on to the lawn. A piece of skull bone was dislodged and floated along the river of red to the bloodfall, starkly white in the sunlight.

"Regular chip off the old block," the half-breed muttered, whirling around to aim the Winchester across the saloon.

CHAPTER NINE

LAINE was framed by the doorway giving on to the rear of the hotel, his bare shoulders and chest slick with sweat in the sunlight shafting in through the front entrance. The man was transfixed by fear for stretched seconds: captured by the hooded-eyed stare of Edge. The half-breed's mouth was compressed into a tight line of cruelty that was some how more menacing than the mizzle hole of the pointing Winchester. But then the tense, straining, mind-bursting moments of evil ended: curtailed by the cracking of Edge's lips to show an ice-cold grin.

"Live frugally from now, feller," he warned. "Because you're doing it on borrowed time."

Laine had to force a lump from his throat before he could speak. The grin that accompanied the words was as bleak as a mountain winter. "You got nothing to fear this side of the river, mister," he rasped. "Corners ain't about to give anyone in town five grand for turning you in."

More citizens of Hate came in through the doorway behind the bar and Laine moved along to the gap.

"You might still figure to get something for walking me across that bridge out there," Edge replied softly, but lowered the rifle to hang loosely in a one-handed grip at his side. The act was proof he did not believe it himself.

"Ain't nothing will satisfy Corners' ache for revenge now, mister," Laine said earnestly, talking as much to the men and women crowding into the saloon behind him as to Edge. "Short of swinging as many of us from those gallows as it takes to cure what ails him."

"Guess a town called Hate just has to be full of hangups," the half-breed murmured wryly.

He swung around to look out into the street again as the town's citizens filed into the saloon from the rear. Not all of them, for three, armed with rifles, stood surveillance duty. Like Edge, they watched the lumber mill, the tall building throwing a foreshortened shadow as the sun climbed toward its noon peak. Nothing moved over there. except the giant water wheel rotating slowly on its axis: and the occasional flick of a tail as the horses in the wagon traces swatted at flies.

"That everybody?" Laine asked when the scraping of bootleather and chair legs against the floorboards had subsided.

The half-breed glanced fleetingly over his shoulder and saw that the shirtless man had an earnestly attentive audience arrayed before him. Men and women, some nursing small babies, and children, either stood or sat in expectant silence. Cyrus McNally had taken his place behind the bar, but in spite of the heat, nobody wanted a drink.

"All of us," Burgess confirmed. "Apart from the men watching the mill."

The storekeeper was clutching a brown paper bag that looked as if it might be stuffed with the collection money. But he refused to meet Edge's quizzical gaze to confirm or deny the tacit query.

"That's good," Laine said, and cleared his

throat: in the manner of man unused to public speaking about to make a speech.

But the sound of hoofbeats—not too far away—interrupted his opening. There were shouts from the watching sentries. Edge swung around and leaned foward to look toward the lumber mill. A lone rider, crouched low in the saddle, galloped his horse from the side of the mill, streaking toward the open gates in the fence. He made a dust-billowing turn on to the trail, heading west across the long strip of valley ravaged of trees. No shots were sent toward him, either from the town or the mill.

"What's happening?" a man in the saloon demanded, alarmed.

The hoofbeats faded into the heat-waved distance.

"One of the deputies just took off," Edge supplied, looking at the mill. Only the wheel and the horses' tails moved. "West."

"Gone to get some help!" a woman put in fearfully.

This triggered a buzz of nervous conversation.

"Not a hope, unless we give him time to get to Trasker and back," Laine snapped across the noise, silencing it. "He ain't gonna cover no sixty miles in what's left of the day."

There was a murmuring of agreement. Then a man's voice was raised. "What we gonna do before he gets back with some more hired guns, Laine?"

"That's what I called this meeting for," the bare-chested man answered as Edge swung around and leaned against the doorframe. "We gotta make a decision and the whole town's gotta do it. Too big for the Citizens Committee to handle on its own. Now, we either gotta talk ourselves out of the

120

spot we're in. Or we gotta smash Luke Corners once and for all."

He paused and there was a long period of hot silence. The mass of faces in front of him presented a blank wall of apprehension that appeared to offer no hope of a breach in the way of positive reaction to Laine's alternatives. Earlier, with the fire of their own anger burning more fiercely than the high sun, their response to Laine's leadership had been spontaneous. Now, with time to think, they were less inclined to wilful recklessness. The scent of the putrefying dead infiltrated the saloon through the open doors and down the stairway.

"Seems to me there ain't no choice, Laine," a man said to puncture the brittle silence. "You said it yourself. We give him the chance, Corners is gonna string some of us up."

Agreement was not entirely unanimous this time.

"That's why I don't want to influence you," Laine replied. "Sure as hell I'd be one of the first to hang."

"Me and Bess'd be in line right behind you," one of Dorrie's former captors said sourly.

"I ain't for nothin' hasty," the old man with a bandage on his bald head whined. "Countin' Miss Dorrie, there's eight people holed up in the mill."

"Seven," Laine corrected. "One just left."

"Okay," the old man allowed with a wave of his mottled hands. "But they got everythin' goin' for 'em. I seen the rack of rifles up in Mr. Corners' living quarters. What we got? Handful of Winchesters and a few handguns. And there's a lot of open ground between the fence and the mill."

"All true," Laine agreed. "If it was easy to smash

121

Corners, guess we'd have done it long ago. Needed the stranger here to kinda set things rolling."

"So let him finish it," the old man said heatedly. "Ain't caused nothin' but trouble since he come to town."

All heads swung toward Edge, who was rolling another cigarette. In the expectant silence, he returned their attention with a cold stare as he ran the gummed strip of paper along his tongue.

"Alex Burgess's got the money collected up," the old man continued. "Man didn't oughta mind stickin' his neck out for a thousand dollars."

Edge struck a match and fired the cigarette. "Working on it, folks, " he said softly. "And next time somebody wrecks my play, I'll kill him."

He spat.

"No!" Laine snapped. "He already tried and I don't like his methods. I told the stranger we're obliged to him. He brought us to our senses. Showed us Corners ain't no God. But if we're gonna have a showdown with him, we'll do it our way. If any of us get killed, it'll be because we called the shots."

"Don't have to call them," Edge muttered. "They'll just come at you of their own accord, like."

"All in favor of a showdown?" Laine asked into the silence which followed the half-breed's comment.

Some hands thrust into the air fast. Others went up more slowly, after surreptitious glances to left and right. Eventually, the upraised arms—some of them shaking—were thicker than the pine trees crowded into the timber-rich valley.

"Against?" Laine asked.

The old man with the head wound was first into the air with his arm. His embarrassed young wife, nursing two babies on her knees, gave a nod of agreement. A dozen or so other women registered their votes, despite the low-voiced disapproval of their men.

Laine didn't smile. "Looks like we smash Corners," he said softly.

"Billy!" the old man behind the bar exclaimed suddenly, like somebody erupting from a trance. His frightened eyes raked the faces of the people in the saloon. "Where's my son?"

"Last time I saw him, he was helping me dig the graves," the pink-faced preacher replied mournfully. He had not voted one way or the other. "Then the marshal spoke to him."

"Colman give him some money," Edge supplied. "For setting me up to get arrested."

A moment of horror gripped the elder McNally, but then he sighed and showed a wan smile. "Out of town is the safest place to be today," he muttered.

"I seen him go, Cyrus," the lone male objector to the showdown with Corners said. "Took off to the north. Reckon he circled around through the trees on the valley slope and waded the water upstream. Didn't wanna run into those gunslingers Miss Dorrie brought back from Trasker."

"Don't care which way he went," McNally murmured, "long as he's out of this." He looked earnestly across the heads of the audience toward Edge. "Don't hold it against him, Mister. Colman must have tricked my boy. Billy don't mean no harm to no one. He's to be pitied."

123

Edge nodded. "Colman's heart sure bled for him," he replied wryly.

"Forget Billy," Laine said harshly. "Now the decision's made, we gotta figure a way to get into the mill."

Amid the almost solid support of his fellow-citizens, Burgess had lost his nervousness. His voice was strong with a determined tone: "Divide up the ammunition from the gun we have, wait until nightfall and then rush them," he proclaimed.

Laine nodded. "Thinking along those lines myself, Mr. Burgess."

Edge dropped his cigarette and trod heavily on it with the heel of his boot.

"That an opinion, stranger?" Laine demanded.

"Plan sounds fine," the half-breed replied evenly. "Should give me plenty of dead men for cover when I go to blast Corners personally."

The attention of the people in the saloon was abruptly switched from the bare-chested man to the half-breed.

"You got any better ideas?" Laine challenged heatedly.

"Maybe."

"Do no harm to listen."

Edge curled back his lips to show a cold grin. "Cost you that thousand dollars."

There was a ripple of shaking heads and a murmuring of more vocal objections. Laine brought silence to the room again.

"I don't buy nothing 'til I know what it is," he posed.

"Glad to hear you're smarter than the way you been acting and talking," the half-breed said.

The taunt erupted anger on the rugged, young

124

face. But the memory of Edge's speed caused Laine to force back the rage. "Spell it out, stranger!"

Edge came away from the doorframe, leaving the rifle where it rested. He strolled casually among the people sitting at the tables. All eyes followed his apparently aimless wandering. But he had an end in view, as men and women shrank back from him, sensing from close quarters the latent cruelty residing in the tall, lean killer.

"Mister, I didn't mean nothin'," the old man with the bandaged head whined as Edge towered over him.

The half-breed ignored him, and moved on toward the bar. The stink of sweating bodies was a stale fetidness in the hot air. "Wouldn't want Corners to hear what I have in mind," Edge said softly as he turned and rested his back against the bar.

The people waited in complete, straining silence. Edge made as if to scratch his right ear. The action began slowly, but abruptly his arm was a blur. His hand closed around the handle of the razor and drew it. A mass gasp of horror swept the room. The preacher gave a strangled cry. Edge had swung toward him and rested the blade of the razor along the top lip of the pink-faced man: sharpened side a hairsbreadth from slicing into the base of the snub nose. The half-breed did not touch him in any other way: the menace of the smooth steel, sufficient to freeze the victim into immobility.

"You can breathe," Edge invited softly. "For awhile."

Twin blooms of dull mist began to spread and fade across the shiny surface of the blade immediately beneath the flaring and contracting nostrils.

"What the hell. . . .?" Laine demanded.

The preacher was speechless, his lips seemingly sealed by dried saliva while his round eyes were held wide enough to pop the balls from the sockets. Sweat stood out on his face like fresh rain beading a rock.

"Figure you'd have the preacher man on the Citizens Committee?" Edge posed, his glinting eyes fixed on the terrified stare of the padre.

"You figure right," Laine answered. "And you oughta know I've got a sixgun aimed at your back. So say what you have to."

"Somebody told a Corners' deputy Maclean was heading out to find me last night," the half-breed said evenly. "Decided at the secret committee meeting, weren't it?"

Stunned silence greeted the rhetorical query. McNally broke it.

"That's right, Laine," the old man said excitedly. "Stranger told me earlier we had a tale-carrier on the committee. Didn't have no chance to pass it on, with what happened."

This produced a ripple of ugly murmurings.

"Why's it have to be the preacher?" a man demanded.

"Don't have to be," Edge answered off-handedly. "But unless you fellers on the committee figure out who it is, I'm gonna start carving."

"A man of God?" a woman gasped.

"Just a man to me, ma'am," the half-breed replied. "I don't have the faith no more. Figure to live in a town like Hate you folks must still have it." He grinned into the sweat-run face. "Guess the preacher's counting on it."

"Leave him be!" a woman shrieked, and

126

knocked over her chair as she leapt from it. "He's the traitor!"

Edge swung around, still keeping the razor tight against the preacher's nose. The old man with the bandaged head was cringing in his chair, seemingly pressed down into it by the weight of enraged stares turned toward him. The heaviest pressure of hatred was directed at him from the blazing eyes of his wife as she clutched her babies to her breasts.

"He'll do anything for money except work!" she snarled. "He fixed it so his number only went into Corners' bag every couple of weeks. Fixed it by letting one of the deputies know about secret meetings. Informing on folk. The other deputies paid him for letting them into our house: into our bedroom." She began to sob. Dry sobs because the hate in her eyes wouldn't let the tears out. "I had to. To buy things for the babies."

"No!" the old man shrieked, lunging for his wife. But she backed away and strong hands captured the man's quaking shoulders and fastened him back on the chair. His terrified gaze swung frantically about the room. It found only acrimony. "You saw. Today wasn't the first time. I'm always gettin' beat up by Mr. Corners men!"

"To make it look good!" his wife accused.

"Pardon me, preacher," Edge said as he removed the razor from the man's flesh. The man slumped back against the bar.

"You still use lousy methods, mister," Laine told Edge. "But sometimes they work."

He levelled his revolver at the quaking old man, who was held fast to the chair by naked terror as his captors and the others around him backed suddenly away. But despite Laine's revulsion for the

127

traitor, he could not bring himself to squeeze the trigger of the revolver. Not in cold blood.

The half-breed moved fluidly away from the bar and while Laine and the old man stared at each other, all the rest of the people in the saloon watched Edge. He halted silently at the rear of the chair and the razor flashed in a sideways stabbing action. The point sank into the soft, pulsing flesh beneath the ear, angling upwards. The blade penetrated smoothly through skin, flesh, muscle. It nicked the brain and the old man died with a sigh. He toppled to the side, drawing himself off the killing weapon. Blood splashed vividly and the flies droned in for the feast.

"Personal," Edge said softly, stooping to wipe the blade on the dead man's shirt sleeve. "He almost got me killed."

"Whoever would have thought it of Mr. Heinz," a woman gasped.

"Fact is, he spilled the beans," the half-breed muttered as he slid the razor back into the neck pouch.

"He was all kinds of a bastard!" the dead man's wife snarled, and spat down on to the corpse.

"I reckon at least fifty-seven varieties," Edge replied softly.

CHAPTER TEN

EDGE sold the citizens of Hate on his plan to get inside the lumber mill across the river. But there was a condition: that the cash would be paid on delivery, not in advance.

Edge raised no objection to this and the meeting broke up, the people filing out the way they had come in, to disperse to their homes and wait for nightfall. Cooking fires were lit, but it was the aroma of coffee that permeated the heat waved air. For with the sickly sweet scent of fast-rotting human flesh pervading the town, few could face food.

The half-breed was not effected in this way, unmindful of the slumped corpse of the traitor as he ate the meal cooked by Cyrus McNally. Finished, he leaned back in the chair and tipped his new hat forward over his eyes. He snored quietly and regularly as the afternoon ground its stifling course, the merciless sun dipping toward the white-peaked mountains in the west and pointing an accusing finger of shadow at the town from the tall mill.

"Rider acomin' fast!"

The excited shout jerked Edge out of sleep. As always, he was instantly aware of his surroundings. His hooded eyes raked the saloon and discovered everything precisely the way it had been when he last saw it. Even McNally seemed not to have moved, held like a statue at the bar, elbows leaning

129

on the counter top, chin in hands and eyes staring into an infinity of sadness.

"Two men on the one horse!" the sentry outside yelled.

This second report brought Edge out of his chair and the old bartender was snapped from his period of mournful reflection. The half-breed reached the vantage point of the open doorway long before McNally had shuffled into position beside him. The two men riding tandem were a half-mile out on the trail bisecting the strip of open ground featured by the stumps of felled pines. The horse was galloping at full-stretch, pumping hooves kicking up a great cloud of dust that billowed out behind like grey smoke. The dark shape of the horse and its two riders were clearly silhouetted against the lighter colored background. But they were not recognizable until they were much closer, racing for the bridge with no slackening of speed.

"Hold your fire!" McNally shrieked: then lunged out into the street, thrusting his thin arms high into the air.

Three rifles cracked, spewing death from the doorway and two windows of the tall mill building. McNally had been facing down the street, addressing his plea to the men watching the mill. He was hit in the back, three red blossoms of oozing blood issuing from a close grouping at the top of his spine. They had merged into a single stain before his falling body smashed his face into the dust. Dying nerves twitched his frail form once and he was still.

"Some guys just won't be told," the half-breed muttered, returning his attention to the approaching riders, looking across the backs of the six horses still hitched to the rail in front of the hotel.

In the saddle was the deputy who had galloped out for the trees that morning. Clinging on to him from behind was Billy McNally. As the horse swerved in through the gateway of the mill, Edge swung up the Winchester. Then, as he was about to lean out for a clear shot, another rifle cracked. Splinters of wood exploded from the doorframe only inches from his head. He whirled, aiming across the street to the figure of Laine in the doorway of the courthouse.

"Billy's on that horse!" the handsome young man yelled angrily.

The animal with its two riders galloped into the cover of the mill building. Edge, his face a mask of cold anger, forced his muscles to relax, starting with those in his finger curled around the trigger. "You got a second mortgage on your life, feller," he called tonelessly.

"I said," Laine reiterated distinctly. "That Billy McNally was on that horse."

"It was him I figured to blast," Edge replied flatly.

"For what?"

"Because I don't reckon such a simple-minded feller like him deserves what he's gonna get from Corners."

Edge could only see Laine. But he sensed many other ears straining to catch his words. And he guessed that every person who heard felt the same degree of horror as Laine showed on his ruggedly handsome face. The man stared at the half-breed in silence for long seconds—until a piercing scream from inside the mill broke the tension.

131

"Why do you always have to be right, mister?" Laine challenged in a snarling tone.

Edge shrugged and showed an icy grin. "A man's got to have one redeeming feature," he replied.

Laine spat.

"McNally!" The voice of Luke Corners trembled against the air of the dying afternoon with a note of triumph giving it power.

"McNally ain't with us no more!" Laine shouted in reply. "Your boys just killed him."

"Pa!" Billy shrieked in anguish. Then was abruptly silent.

Corners kept the peace for a few moments, then broke it. "To bad! Still, it don't matter! Everyone in town likes Billy, don't they?" He paused, but no voices filled it. "Of course they do," he continued. "Nothing about the addle-brain idiot to dislike!" He injected harshness into his voice now. "Whereas that trouble-making drifter! Why, he's the cause of everything that's happened here today. Everyone'll benefit if you turn him over to me in exchange for Billy. And I'll take it as a sign of your good faith that nothing like it will ever happen again. Forgive and forget! What d'you say?"

"Can't tell you, Corners!" Laine shouted. "Too many ladies around." He lowered his voice. "You still ready to do it, stranger?" he hissed at Edge.

"Takes a lot to make me change my mind," the half-breed replied in the same low tone.

"You want Billy McNally to suffer?" Corners yelled, his voice short on confidence now.

"We ain't sure he's still in one piece to do any suffering!" Laine challenged.

Another pause, and then Billy's voice shouted from the mill. It had a pained tone. "Bastard deputy booted me in the balls when I tried to run, Mr. Laine. I was tricked out at the cabin. Deputy told me Pa was sick."

He tried to go on, but a hand or a gag muffled him into silence.

"Good enough, Laine?" Corners yelled.

"I wanna see him!"

Again the demand drew many seconds of silence from the mill as the sun sank lower behind it, beginning to become tinged with red. Then.

"Be a pleasure, Laine!"

The pause without voices was longer this time, unevenly paced by the sound of heavy footfalls within the mill.

"Going upstairs," Laine rasped across the street at Edge.

The half-breed nodded and remained in the cover of the doorway, canting the barrel of the Winchester slightly.

"Here he is, Laine!" Corners roared. "So you can see the bullets tearing him apart if the drifter don't show pretty damn quick."

A loft hatchway was exposed above the main door of the mill and the wooden jib of a crane was swung out. A chain hung from the pulley, the hook at its end looped under Billy's belt at the back. The man swung in a circle, his legs hanging down as he forced his torso and head up, forming a right-angle at the waist. His arms were stretched out in a silent plea for help.

"Get that drifter out on to the street!" Corners bellowed.

Edge moved while Corners was shouting, lunging from the doorway to crouch among the horses. The animals snorted and tried to rear, but were held down by the hitched reins. The half-breed saw Billy's position for the first time between the flanks of two excited horses. He aimed and fired at the precise moment the men at the mill opened up. Two of the horses keeled over and one sat down. Animal blood gushed into the dust. Billy was hit between the eyes as he swung around to take his last look at the town he had always wanted to leave. A fraction of an instant later the lead burrowed into his brain and he was gone forever. Rising dust from the lashing hooves of the surviving horses and the writhing bodies of the injured animals covered Edge's first steps across the street. But then his running form was in full view and the rifles cracked. He threw himself forward, tucking his chin to his chest and powering into a head-over-heels roll. Bullets whined around him and spat up divots of dry earth. His heels thudded to the ground and he lunged upright: then dived full-length through the doorway into the courthouse.

Laine stepped deftly out of his way and the shooting stopped. He glanced quickly out through the doorway and withdrew. "Billy's dead," he reported flatly.

"There's a lot of it about today," Edge replied, hauling himself to his feet and dusting himself off. "Almost happened to me—just crossing the street."

Laine met the piercing stare of the slitted blue eyes and tried to shrug off his nervousness. "We can't afford to waste lead with covering fire," he excused.

The sunlight shafting in through the west-facing windows of the courthouse was less harsh and carried a definite tinge of red as afternoon faded into evening. The temperature was still as high as ever, but Laine was certain he felt cold enough to shiver as the half-breed moved towards him, the rifle levelled.

"I ask for any?" The words were hissed through clenched teeth, the thin lips hardly moving.

"Guess not."

Edge worked the lever action of the Winchester. "When I ask a man for something and he don't deliver, that's when I get mean with him." He slammed the rifle stock into his shoulder and snapped a shot through the doorway. Pumped the action and fired again. "I'm almost never mean to animals," he muttered.

Laine leaned to the side to look around the tall half-breed and saw the final nervous twitches of the two horses put out of their agony. The three surviving animals sidled away to the extent of their hitched reins, and became quiet.

"Everyone ready?"

Laine dragged his thoughtful gaze away from the inert horseflesh and gave a curt nod. "Just waiting for the word. Tell me something?"

Edge began to take shells from his gunbelt and push them through the gate of the Winchester. He grinned. "What's a nice guy like me doing in a business like this?" he suggested wryly.

Laine did not seem to be the kind of man to have a sense of humor at the best of times. "Killing Billy and then the horses . . . did you feel any different about it?"

"Sure," the half-breed replied. "With the horses, I felt I was doing them a favor."

Suspicion narrowed Laine's dark eyes. "Billy, too," he reminded.

"Sure," Edge allowed indifferently as he finished the reloading and rasped a hand across his stubbled jaw. "As well as."

"As well as what?"

"As well as the fact that the stupid lunkhead almost got me arrested." He altered his mouthline a trifle, to form the grin into one of cunning. "And as well as another fact—that maybe Corners could have talked you into exchanging me for the loony." He spat out through the doorway.

"You ever do anything that don't have an angle to it, mister?" Laine asked bitterly.

"Yeah," Edge replied. "Sometimes I pitch a curve."

CHAPTER ELEVEN

Two hours after full nightfall the moon was big and bright. It reflected against the unlit windows of the quiet mill and turned the river to molten silver. The folded body of Billy McNally suspended from the crane jib was an obscene silhouette, evilly still. The town was as silent as the mill but the smell of death was stronger for it was host to the rotting bodies of six men and three horses. There was not even the hint of a breeze to waft away the nauseating odor. The humid heat continued unabated in the meeting of the valleys. Only the monotonously slow churning of the water mill had disturbed the peace since the explosion of shots which had killed the wounded horses.

But to the men wading upstream from the south the quiet sounds of their progress seemed to echo stridently between the tree-clad slopes of the valley. There were fifteen of them and they had left town immediately the red sun plunged behind the distant mountain crests: stalking off into the trees flanking the disused eastern trail. Laine took the lead, with Edge close behind him and the others strung out at the rear.

They swung south, up the timber-rich valley slope and then west, on a parallel course with the single street of Hate. All were on foot and armed with a motley assortment of conventional and unorthodox weapons. Edge had his rifle, revolver

137

and razor: Laine carried a Winchester and two men had handguns. The remainder had scoured the basements, lofts and closets of their houses in search of the tools they had used in the free enterprise days before Luke Corners established his grip of iron on the town. Thus, the majority of the men moving through the night carried axes, saws, sledgehammers, knives and even bundles of old dynamite sticks.

The men headed into the southern section of the valley for almost a quarter of a mile, before crossing the river at a point where the pine grew thick to both banks. They stayed in the river to move north toward the mill, crouching low to keep under the bank. At first, the cool water served to negate the heat of their bodies as it lapped around their lower legs. But as they neared the looming shape of the high mill building the sweat of tension began to pump from their pores again.

Only two pairs of eyes followed their progress as the stealthy attackers approached their objective. Two men armed with Winchesters were sprawled full-length on the courthouse roof, fingers curled around the triggers of their rifles. Over in the hotel and behind the cover of the bank, other men waited in sweating ignorance of what was happening. Tacky hands gripped rifles and revolvers loaded with no more than two or three rounds of shared-out ammunition. Their ears strained unnecessarily to hear the crack of gunfire from the courthouse roof which would signal the start of the diversionary action.

The women and children, under the apprehensive guardianship of the pink-faced preacher, waited in tense silence in the store of Alex Burgess.

The two dogs prowled nervously, with hair bristling and snouts sniffing the death-sweet, tension-laden, heat-heavy air. Horses stood in statue-like immobility, ears pricked and nostrils flared.

The men on the courthouse roof saw the leading figure of the column in the river wade past the end of the fence marking the extent of the mill property. The others moved slowly in his wake. Closer to the building, where the rotating wheel caused the silvered smoothness of the slow-running river to bubble into white foam, some of the men snaked up on the bank. Their shadowed forms became merged with the stacks of fresh-cut logs and sawn timber littering the fenced property behind the building. A group of three men stayed in the water and moved cautiously along the side of the mill toward the churning wheel.

A match flared briefly in the deep shadow where the side of the mill met the river bank.

"That's it!" one of the men on the courthouse roof rasped.

But the whispered words were drowned by the crack of the other man's rifle. An instant of silence fled into time past and then the men below responded to the signal. Pent-up excitement ripped from throats as if to give added power to the bullets which were exploded toward the mill.

Edge was crouched at the side of a large heap of logs. The barrage of shots which thudded lead into the side of the mill acted as a spur to drive him forward. Together with other attackers, he sprinted for the rearing wall of the mill as the men inside shouted in alarm and returned the fusillade of shots with one of their own.

It was up to each individual man now. The half-breed's plan had begun with the stealthy exodus from the far end of town and ended with the opening barrage of covering fire. He could have extended it beyond this point, given a knowledge of the mill's interior layout which most of the lumber men knew. But this was no well-drilled army unit tractable to discipline. It was a mob tasting freedom after many years in a vicious yoke.

The fire from across the river cost no lives. It was aimed high to avoid scything into the attackers and did no more damage than digging splinters of wood from the soutly-built mill wall. The dynamite made a far greater impression. The match which had signalled the opening shots of the battle had set light to the fuse of four sticks lashed together. This lethal bundle was hurled high up the wall of the mill. The thrower and his two companions ducked under the water and the dynamite exploded with an ear-splitting roar.

Midway along the rear wall of the mill, another flaring fuse found its mark and a second explosion masked the crackle of gun fire. Blazing and blackened timber flashed through the air inside and outside the mill as the men on the town side of the river expended their meagre supplies of ammunition.

The first man to die in the battle was the one who had set the charge at the rear of the building. The ancient fuse burned too fast and he had retreated only two yards when the dynamite went off. Blast picked him off his feet like tumbleweed in a high wind and hurled him against a pile of prepared fence poles. A dozen cruelly pointed lengths of wood skewered his body and burst out at the back. Blood fountained away from his burst flesh like red mud through a sieve.

"Rob's dead!" a man shrieked in horror.

"Staked his all and lost," Edge muttered as he slid around the corner of the mill on the side away from the river.

With shouts and the crackle of gunfire filling the night, seeming insignificant after the two mighty explosions, he reached the far corner and moved along the front of the building toward the main doorway. At the rear, lumber men sprinted toward the gaping hole as the smoke cleared. On the river side of the mill, the three men grasped the paddles of the water wheel and were carried up toward the second jagged aperture ripped in the wall.

The big double doors at the front of the building were solidly closed and the half-breed crouched down at the side of a window. He peered inside and there was nobody to see him. For many seconds had passed since the final shot was fired from the town and the defenders were re-positioning themselves to meet the attack from another quarter.

Edge's hooded eyes saw a great cavern of a place, revealed in the flickering light of many fires where blazing debris from the explosions had ignited wood shavings and discarded chippings. The first floor was two stories high for the greater part of its dirt-floored area, with piles of logs provoding ample cover. At second floor level there was a broad balcony around all four walls, supporting stacks of timber cut into building planks. At one side was an endless belt split into two sections and driven by the churning water wheel. The enormous blade of a circular saw was stationary halfway along the belt, its vicious teeth gleaming in the firelight. The furnace box of the steam engine glowed with hot ashes but the latent power of the boiler was not connected with the piston to drive the giant saw.

The half-breed spotted two deputies and one hired gun crouched behind timber stacks; their rifles aimed at the hole ripped in the rear close to where the stairway from the balcony reached ground level. Four lumbermen charged in through the jagged aperture, their axes and sledgehammers held high and their mouths wide to scream aloud their fury. Gunfire exploded and three of the invaders were hurled to the floor with chests blossoming red. The fourth threw himself into cover at the foot of the stairway, yelling for those behind him to stay back.

Up on the balcony, the first man stepped in off the water wheel. A gunslinger moved out of the shadows, thrust his rifle into the intruder's stomach and squeezed the trigger. The lumber man crumpled. The attacker immediately behind him stepped off the wheel before the gunslinger could pump a new shell into the breech. The rifle jabbed at him and the lumber man toppled backwards with a scream. The strident sound was curtailed by the evil crunch of crushed bones as the live body was fed into the massive cogs linking the wheel with the drive to the belt.

Something metallic flashed at the shadowed area beneath the foot of the stairs. The axe spun through the firelit air like an Indian tomahawk and the gunslinger on the balcony screamed. The blade cleaved deep into his back and he staggered forward. The third man who had used the water wheel to enter, stepped to the side, plucked the Winchester from the loose grip of the dying man and kicked him on his way. He was dead when he splashed into the river below.

Edge stepped in front of the window and began to blast through it. Glass sprayed across the dirt floor and bullets homed in on their targets. He heard a shout of encouragement for the men outside to charge in. He saw the two deputies and the gunslinger take his bullets in their flesh, dropping where they were hit, with no more life left in them to turn around and see who had killed them. The half-breed waited until the lumber men began to duck in through the back before he followed his bullets, diving through the glassless window and rolling: then bellying into the cover of a stack of timber. Bullets spatted into the ground close to him, jerking up small showers of dirt. The shots came from up above and his slitted eyes raked the balcony. Most of it was in heavy shadow, out of reach of the light from the dancing flames.

Another burst of gunfire forced him to duck, but he had the man spotted. He waited for the barrage to stop, then flung himself upright, swinging the Winchester to the aim. But he was too late. The lumber man on the balcony had beaten him to the kill, creeping up behind the gunslinger and smashing down with the sledgehammer he carried. The rifleman died without a sound, his body still folded into a crouch as he fell from behind his cover of planks. The big head of the hammer had smashed through his skull and been buried in the pulpy, red bubbling mess beneath. The man who had struck the killing blow leapt forward to grasp the handle.

"I showed him, didn't I?" he boasted joyously. A gunshot cracked and the man's right eye exploded in a shower of blood. He was flung back against the planks, then bounced forward and toppled off the balcony to crash to the floor.

"Pride comes before a fall," Edge muttered as he whirled to locate the gunman.

For long moments, as the wheel churned and the fires crackled, he saw no sign of movement. Even the men who had poured through the hole in the rear wall were not in sight. But then he heard running footfalls and snapped his head around. The gunslinger who had done all the talking was racing along between two stacks of logs. He was minus rifle and revolver and his once hard face was now twisted into a mask of terror. Behind him in the timber-flanked aisle sprinted two lumbermen, axes held high and mouths wide to yell their triumph. Ahead of the fleeing gunslinger, as a lumber man rose at each side, a two-handed saw was lifted six inches from the ground. The terrified fugitive did not see the obstacle. He screamed as the wicked teeth bit through his flesh to scrape against the ankle bones. He pitched full-length to the dirt floor. His pursuers stopped short, dropped to their knees and swung down the big axes. One blade sank into the helpless man's back, going all the way through to pin him to the earth. He was dead before the second axe smashed through the back of his head to splash great gouts of blood on to the timber at either side.

"Did we kill that bastard!" one of the axe wielders yelled in delight.

"Sure gave him the chop," Edge replied wryly, raking his glint-eyed gaze around the great cavern of the mill.

Both deputies and the quartet of hired guns

144

were dead. But Luke Corners and his niece had been noticeably absent from the scene of the slaughter.

"Maybe they sneaked out the same way we left town," Laine rasped from the rear of the mill.

"Way to find out!" Another man roared, running out from cover to reach the controls of the big steam engine. "Blow this damn mill to bits. If they're in here, they'll show when this baby starts building up a nice head of steam."

He threw the lever to set the piston throbbing and the saw blade whirling. Then he began to frantically hurl cord wood into the furnace box.

"No!" Dorrie shrieked from high in the building. "Let me get out!"

Her footfalls clattered on the stairway, increasing in volume as she raced downwards. Her dress was a blur of white on the balcony and then she appeared clearly on the final flight down to ground level. The man feeding the furnace continued with his self-imposed chore working with the frenetic speed of a mind crazed by power. Edge and the other half-dozen survivors of the attacking force watched the woman coldly.

"Bitch!" Laine spat at Dorrie as she reached the foot of the stairway and became transfixed by the stares of the men.

"I'll do anything!" she pleaded, pathetic in her helplessness. Her face was stark white against the soiled dressing on her cheek wound.

"I reckon you would," Laine snarled at her.

"Just one thing," a man said icily as running footfalls pounded on the bridge outside.

Dorrie swallowed hard. "Yes?" she forced out.

"Die!" the man snapped, and hurled a knife toward her.

The blade thudded home beneath the thrusting swell of her left breast. The woman screamed once and raised her hands to grip the quivering handle. But she died before she touched it and crumpled into a heap: all white except for her black hair and the expanding stain of red from the wound.

"Guess that's the first time she ever did like she was told," somebody said as shoulders crashed against the big doors at the front of the mill.

As the doors burst open and men and women slammed the box closed and shut off the outlet valve. The engine hissed furiously and began to tremble on its mountings.

Edge turned toward Alex Burgess, who was among the first to stagger in through the doorway. His voice rapped out clearly above the racket of the racing engine.

"Obliged for bringing along the money, feller," he said, aware of a movement up on the balcony as he reached out for the paper sack in the storekeeper's hands.

Burgess made to give it to him.

"No!" Laine commanded.

The handsome young man, still shirtless, his sweat-sheened upper body streaked with soot and blood, stepped up to the engine controls and opened the safety valve. He waited for the initial rush of steam to subside.

"We need the mill," he announced to all who looked at him. Then he fixed his steady gaze on the half-breed's coldly impassive face. "And all the money we've got. We'll pay you ten dollars for your plan, mister. You didn't do no more than the

146

rest of us, and Luke Corners is still alive. We'll take care of him ourselves."

Burgess began to withdraw his offer of the sack. Behind him, the vast majority of the townspeople gave tacit approval to Laine's contention. Edge's hooded eyes moved in their sockets to look at the survivors of the battle. Still breathing raggedly from the exertion and tension, they showed their readiness to swing their blood-dripping weapons to menace the half-breed.

A new movement high on the balcony scratched a faint impression on the periphery of Edge's vision: but his impassive features gave not the slightest sign that anything was wrong. Then, to a gasp from the watchers, he whirled to the left and the Winchester canted and bucked in his hands. Laine's rifle and the axes, hammers and saws of the other men started to menace Edge. Then the familiar twin reports of Corners' shotgun shattered the second of silence which followed the crack of the Winchester. The buckshot spattered harmlessly into the high roof as the old man's massive body plummeted downwards. He had taken the bullet in the shoulder, but the impact of his head against the hard planks beneath the endless belt plunged him into unconsciousness. His inert body was carried inexorably toward the blurred serration of the spinning blade.

The eyes of every man and woman except Edge stared in horrified fascination as the cruel teeth of the saw ripped into the top of Corners' head and slashed through his skull as if it were made of cardboard. A drenching spray of crimson with highlights of gleaming white fragments of bone spumed away from the ghastly path of the blade as it sliced

147

the rugged face in two and then began to bisect the body.

Some men crouched down and started to vomit. Many women covered their eyes as others crushed the faces of their children against them to hide the awesome sight. But most seemed to be frozen into a state of suspended animation which did not end until the blade burst free after severing the old man's right leg. The two halves of the split body rolled on to their sides.

It was at that moment that Edge snatched the money sack from Burgess's numbed fingers and back-stepped away from the armed men. The store-keeper gasped and spun around. The others swung their wan faces toward the half-breed and saw the Winchester levelled at Laine. Three men took a pace forward, but Laine's voice halted the movement.

"Hasn't there been enough killing? he asked stridently. "If the drifter wants the money that much, let him have it."

"I want it," Edge replied evenly as the endless belt tossed the two halves of the body on to a cushioning heap of sawdust. He circled around to the blasted hole in the rear wall, aware that one of the deputies' horses was hitched out there, still saddled from the ride to bring in Billy McNally. "And what I want, I usually get."

"By one way or another," Laine said bitterly.

"By hook or by crook," Burgess put in mournfully.

"Right," Edge called as he ducked out through the blackened hole. "And sometimes by cutting Corners."